KEEPERS

DAVID THOMAS

ISBN
978-1-956161-32-8 (Paperback)
978-1-956161-31-1 (eBook)

TABLE OF CONTENTS

PROLOGUE

AUGUST 16th, 1981

Patience is not in the vocabulary of one who is only 7 years old. Sean Malone had jumped out of bed that morning at 6am and by 7am he was fully packed and ready to go on his first expedition to the wilderness frontier.

It was now 9:26am and he was still waiting. Mom and Dad were having a "second cup of coffee".

It was an absolutely gorgeous summer day outside their Lewiston, New York 2250 sq ft single story brick home. You could hear what sounded like every bird in upstate New York, out enjoying this perfect day. Standing outside on the back porch and looking south, down the gorge, you could see the mist rising from Niagara Falls.

Lewiston, New York is a small town of approximately 16,000 people situated on the American side of the lower Niagara River where it joins Lake Ontario.

It was a wonderful place to grow up.

Sean was a good looking boy, strong shouldered with an athletic build. His steely blue eyes and soft brown hair accented what would later become a strikingly handsome young man.

At 10:03, he couldn't take it any longer. He went into the kitchen, walked up to the table where his parents were laughing at some unknown (probably stupid) joke and said," Mom! Dad! I know to you there doesn't appear to be any reason to be in a big rush, but if we don't leave soon we won't get to Yellowstone before all the bears in the park go into hibernation."

His father smiled at him and in his most patient voice said," Well there you are son. We've been waiting all morning for you to finish getting ready."

With that Sean rolled his eyes in a showing of complete exasperation and darted out the front door with Reggie, their Jack Russell terrier barking excitedly right on his heels.

Mom and Dad locked up the house, set the the alarm, got in their brand new Jeep Cherokee and pulled out of the driveway headed for what was to be an unforgettable trip.

On the first day they went across the Lewiston-Queenston Bridge, thru a small section of lower Ontario, Canada, entering back into the U.S. at Detroit, Michigan. They continued on around the southern tip of Lake Michigan eventually reaching Chicago where they decided to spend the night at the Marriot Hotel.

It didn't take Sean too long to figure out that they weren't going to make it to Yellowstone by nightfall. Why was Dad driving so slowly?

On day two they got an early start (around 5: am) and headed northwest to I-90 west. It was about this point when his Dad announced that they were coming up on a bridge that crossed the Mississippi River. Sean couldn't believe it. To think they were crossing the "Great Mississippi, Gateway to the wilderness. *(Now we're getting somewhere)*, he thought.

"Dad, can we stop and take a look?" He asked anxiously.

His father looked at his mother and said," Alright, but only for a few minutes. We've got a long way to go to reach Rapid City by nightfall."

He pulled the Jeep over on the opposite side of the bridge at a vista point.

Sean jumped from the car and ran to the metal rail to look down at the river. He was in awe of the pure majesty of the great body of water flowing past him. As he stood there, he couldn't help imagining what it must have been like going down the river in a canoe all the way to New Orleans and the Gulf of Mexico.

His thoughts were broken off suddenly by an odd smell that seemed to be coming from below him down by the waters edge. Reggie, who had come up behind him stopped, sniffed the air and began to growl. Sean slowly looked over the railing down to the shoreline and at first could not comprehend what it was he was looking at. Below him was a huge collection of garbage.

There were beer and soda cans, plastic bags, old diapers, cereal boxes, soap and cleanser containers. Plus what seemed like just about every other type of junk you could think of.

Then to top it off, surrounding this "natural trash bin" was a ring of what looked like oil and soap bubbles. Like an oil slick.

Sean and Reggie both stood there looking down at this mess which was about 70 feet below them, when suddenly he realized that something or someone was looking back up at him from the middle of the mess. He tried to pull his eyes from it but he couldn't seem to do it. It actually seemed to mesmerize him.

His father called to him from back by the car but got no response. He walked over to where his son was and ask in his usual jovial tone," Hey buddy what's up. Couldn't you hear me?"

Sean just stood there looking down. His dad, seeing the curious look on his son's face followed his gaze to the river below and saw the mess.

"What is it?" "What do see," his dad asked.

Before he could say another word the boy bolted from the rail off to the left and started down a trail with Reggie right behind him.

"Hey, where do you think you're going? Sean, come back here."

It was as if the boy couldn't hear him. He kept going until he and the dog got to the bottom. He stood there staring at the mess as his father finally caught up to him and breathing heavily came up along side of him.

"What is it son?"

Sean just went on staring and slowly lifted his arm and pointed. His father followed his outstretched arm until he too could see what had made his son act in such a peculiar manner. In front of them about 10 feet from where they stood he saw it.

There was a pair of eyes just starring into space. Sean's dad looked around and found a pole in the trash pile and used it to drag whatever it was to shore.

It was a dead deer, or more exactly a fawn. It was bloated from being in the water but beside that and the vacant eyes there didn't appear to be anything else wrong with it.

There were no bite marks or signs of mauling.

"What happened to it?" Sean asked.

"I don't know. Maybe it drowned. It almost looks as though it was poisoned but unfortunately we may never know. Let's not mention this to Mom.

You know how she is about animals. Especially baby ones.

"By the way, how'd you see it from all the way up there," he said gesturing up at the vista point high above.

"I don't know Dad, but I could smell it before I could see it," replied Sean.

His dad got a very curious expression on his face. Then shrugging his shoulders and giving him a patronizing grin he reached out and ruffled his son's hair and said," well we better get back before your mother wonders what happened to us".

With that they climbed back up the hill, jumped back into the car and got back on the road headed for Rapid City, South Dakota.

They arrived there at about 7:30 that evening, exhausted from the earlier events of the day and the long drive. They all helped set up camp at the Rapid City KOA campground just a short distance from Mount Rushmore.

Sean was in a hurry to get some sleep so he'd be ready for his first visit to the monument. He had done a lot of reading up on the history of the construction of it and was looking forward to seeing the huge busts of George Washington, Thomas Jefferson, Theodore Roosevelt and Abraham Lincoln.

He got up the next morning at about 7:15 and climbed out of his tent to find his dad already up cooking breakfast. Dad was always up early. He said it was part of his Marine training. He had gone into the Marines shortly after high school on an ROTC program.

He said that was the only way he could afford to go to college at M.I.T. and get a degree in nuclear physics.

While he was in the Marines he learned how to survive in the wilderness with almost nothing. He taught Sean the ability to always be aware of his surroundings and to pay attention to all of his senses and use them to his advantage.

When he heard Sean he turned from the campfire and said," Well, it's the great adventurer appearing from his lair, how about some fresh squeezed orange juice?"

"That sounds great. That bacon smells great."

"It'll be done just about the time you get back from washing your face down at the stream."

Sean grabbed a towel and headed off down the trail with Reggie trotting along right behind him.

It wasn't very far to the stream, only about 150 yards or so. While Sean was washing his face with the clear mountain spring water Reggie was busy trying to drink every drop in the stream. While he was drinking a rainbow trout went swimming by and that was all it took. Reggie got so excited that he was running and jumping around in theicy water and at one point he leaped up on Sean's back as he was bending over to get a drink himself. This forced him forward enough to loose his balance and he fell into the water face first. He was so surprised that he came up spitting and coughing. He sat back on the ground and couldn't help but laugh. He laughed so hard that tears came to his eyes as he watched Reggie bouncing down the steam after the elusive fish.

When the dog finally returned (without the trout) Sean figured it was time to head back. As he stood up he said to Reggie," I think that's about enough exercise. What do you say we get back to camp and get some real breakfast?"

Reggie barked his agreement and they both set off back up the trail. As they walked along the dog ran ahead in a hurry obviously thinking about bacon. Sean was taking his time, trying to smell and feel the forest. As he walked he heard a rustling in the undergrowth and stopped dead in his tracks. He could hear it off to his right but he could also tell that it was a ways off the trail. He slowly walked on the balls of his feet into the brush and after about 15 feet he heard it again. At this point he got down on his hands and knees and crawled ahead. He'd gone about 10 more feet when he gently lifted a branch of a fern and came face to face with the biggest rattle snake he had ever seen.

Now you have to keep in mind that to a 7 year old boy, on his hands and knees looking at a very upset rattle snake from about 15 inches in front of his face, is bound to think that this has got to be the biggest snake in the entire world.

Sean froze like a statue. He was starring at the snake and the snake, coiled up and rattling, was starring at him. As he thought about the fact that here he was, scared to death, he began to realize that the snake had to be just as scared as he was. After what seemed like an eternity the snake seemed to calm. It stopped rattling although it remained coiled looking suspiciously at what it was sure had to be the biggest human it had ever seen. Then it seemed to sense that this human was no threat and slowly uncoiled itself and began to go about its business as though nothing had happened.

It was about then that Sean started to realize that every creature on this planet lived by an unwritten law. It was called survival. Animals, birds, insects and fish all wanted nothing more out of life than survival. The only possible detriment to those goals were the actions of human beings.

Sean made it back to camp in just a few minutes and over breakfast told his parents in detail what had happened during his walk back from the stream. They listened intently to what he told them and when he got to the part about the snake his parents looked at each other in what could only be a knowing glance. His mother, being a botanist, was not frightened at all about his running into a live rattle snake. Many times in her career she had come across all kinds of God's creature and had learned the same basic lesson that had just dawned on her son. She told him," In your life you will hopefully have many opportunities to experience nature in all it's wonder. Don't ever forget that feeling you had when you discovered that we are all on this planet to help each other".

When they were finished with their breakfast they packed up the camp and headed out to see the beautiful Mount Rushmore.

After spending about 3 hours seeing the sights they got back on the road headed for their final destination. Yellowstone National Park, Wyoming.

It was late in the evening when they got into Yellowstone. Sean was so excited that he was sure that he'd never get any sleep. Even setting up camp didn't seem like any problem. After having something to eat they sat for a short while around the campfire and finally Sean could feel his eyelids begin to close. He said his goodnights and gave Mom and Dad a kiss and headed off to his tent. He had no idea what excitement tomorrow would bring. Had he known he may have had more trouble getting to sleep but like all young boys, he dropped off very quickly.

When they all got up the next morning they decided it was time to see all the sights that they driven almost 2000 miles to see. They hopped into their car and began doing the driving tour of Yellowstone.

Dad had a map of the park he had received when they entered last night. They started at the same place that most people probably start. Old Faithfull Geyser. From there they made their way around to the Grand Canyon of Yellowstone. Words cannot describe it. When you stand at the viewpoint and look down into the canyon it actually makes you dizzy.

As they left there they headed for Mammoth Hot Springs where they took the walking tour. As they walked along their tour guide told them that the water that was bubbling up below the platform they were walking on was hot enough to hard boil an egg in four minutes. Now that's hot.

They left there and continued their drive around the park. It was amazing. Almost like going back in time to the old west. They saw buffalo, moose and even bears. It was tempting to roll down the window and try to draw a bear closer with part of the sandwich Mom had made for him but Sean remembered what Dad had told him about not only how dangerous that could be but also how the entire park was such an ecologically balancedenvironment and that it would be unbelievably callous to do anything that could upset that balance. The rangers said that it is so sensitive that it's even forbidden to bring in live bait to fish with in Yellowstone Lake or any of the many steams and rivers within the park. You have to use lures.

By this time it was starting to get late and Mom decided that it was time to find a place to camp for the night. In Yellowstone that's not hard. There are so many campgrounds to choose from. Dad decided to stay at one that was right by Yellowstone Lake. Sean and his dad grabbed their fishing poles and went down to the water to try their luck at catching dinner. It didn't take Sean long to master the art of casting and soon he caught his first fish. It was under 12 inches so was declared a keeper.

In Yellowstone if a caught fish is over 12 inches you must throw it back. This perplexed him until his father explained that this was necessary to ensure that the larger fish were the ones that would spawn, laying their eggs when the time was right thus continuing the cycle of evolution.

After they had caught two more trout they headed back to the camp where Mom, with her expert culinary skills using a variety of natural herbs created a banquet fit for a king, (and a prince).

At dark they all sat around the campfire, roasting marshmallows and listening to the sounds of the forest.

The following morning Sean got up earlier than anyone else. He wanted to go down to the lake and get some fishing in before breakfast. Wouldn't Mom and Dad be surprised when they saw that he had caught breakfast for all of them?

On his way down the path to the lake he past a senior couple out for an early morning trail walk. As Sean past them the man smiled and said," Getting an early start I see."

"Yes sir. I want to surprise my parents."

"Well I'm sure your folks will be impressed," he said.

Sean watched as the couple walked over to a stump and sat down. He then continued on down the path to the water. When he got there he quickly set down his fishing tackle box, opened it and got out what he was sure was the best lure he had. He was sure the fish would agree with him. He attached it to his pole and cast it as far as he could. After waiting the required 5 seconds he began to reel in his line.

As he was reeling in his line he happened to look up the shoreline and about one hundred feet from were he was he noticed a young woman. She looked to be in her early twenties and was dressed in a tank top and pair of cut off jeans. She was carrying something in her hand. Sean continued reeling and watching as he saw her wade out into the water until she was waist deep. He saw her reach down and unscrew a cap on what he could now see was a bottle. She lifted it to her head and as he watched she dumped it on her head. He couldn't believe his eyes when he saw her begin to wash her hair with shampoo. In the middle of Yellowstone Lake. Unbelievable.

It was at this moment that he felt a slight tug on his line and knew he was about to catch his first fish of the day.

At first it felt like a sort of vibration. He looked down at his feet to see if the ground was moving and at that point the vibration began to grow stronger. It was beginning to be more than vibration. More like trembling, and it was getting stronger. Now he could hear it. It was like a rumbling. As the trembling got stronger the sound got louder. It was getting so loud that

Sean thought it might be thunder or an earthquake but when he looked to the sky there wasn't a cloud to be seen. He could hear it and he could feel it but he couldn't imagine what it might be. All he knew was that he could sense the danger.

He turned around and saw the old couple still sitting on the stump, but they weren't looking at him. They were looking to the side. Sean could see their eyes which were as big as saucers. He followed their gaze turning in that direction.

Then he saw it, coming right at him.

CHAPTER 1

April 14th, Present Day
Mammoth Lake, California

Of all the unusual, crazy and sometimes dangerous things he had to do in his line of work, this was quite possibly the worst. Or it sure rated in the top ten. At six feet-one inch tall and 186 pounds Sean Malone's physical build just didn't fit in this tiny crack in the earth. His broad shoulders weren't exactly made to go through an opening that appeared to be about fourteen inches by twenty inches.

He figured that he would just be able to squeeze through by exhaling and pushing hard with his legs. He wasn't normally claustrophobic but something about being in a cave hundreds of feet below the surface that kept getting smaller and smaller gave him the willies.

This particular section looked to be about ten to twelve feet long and beyond it he could feel a slight breeze. All he had to do was get through this tiny opening.

He took a couple of deep breaths, exhaled and lunged forward. He made it about five feet, and was stuck. The only part of his body he could move were his hands, which were stretched out in front of him, and his feet. He tried to wiggle backward. It seemed the more he struggled the tighter he was wedged. Panic began to overtake him and that was causing him to start to hyperventilate. He was sweating even though the temperature was extremely mild.

While he laid there all he could smell was the ammonia odor of bat guano and he knew he was in some very serious trouble. Then he heard it. Their high pitched screeching and their flapping wings. Suddenly everything went dark. All he could do was close his eyes. Then, as quickly as it started it was over. The bats were past him. (*Ok,*) he thought. (*That's a relief, but now what*). He was still stuck.

In front of him he saw a large shadow move across the other side of the opening. It was slowly coming closer. The panic started again and just when he thought he couldn't take it any longer, he heard," aaahh, what's up doc."

"Holy crap Jacob"! Sean yelled. "You scared the hell out of me."

He felt a sudden flood of relief as he realized it was his co-worker and best friend Jacob (Jake) Collins.

"Sean, you know that the only person in the world who can call me Jacob and get away with it is my mother," replied Jake with a very serious look on his face.

"Oh, yeah! Well I'll bet twenty bucks that you'd never scare you're mom like that.

And don't tell me you would. Remember I know your mom and I'm pretty sure she'd box your ears," joked Sean. "I'm also pretty sure she likes me better than you."

"Yeah, you're probably right," replied Jake with a mock frown on his face.

Jake was the same age as Sean, similar in build but a couple of pounds heavier and slightly shorter, with black hair and hazel colored eyes.

He and Sean had played football together at Syracuse University. Sean played halfback and Jake was the fullback. They played so well together that everyone called them zig and zag.

They graduated in the same class, Sean getting his degree in chemical engineering while Jake's degree was in hydro engineering.

After graduation they both took jobs with the Department of the Interior. Then after 9/11, they were absorbed into the Department of Homeland Security.

Their present assignment was investigating a report by Fish and Game about fish and animals dying in the area around Mammoth Lake, California.

When they landed at San Jose International in San Jose, California, after flying from Washington DC on a commercial airliner, they were met by a ranger from the National Parks Service and told that there was a Bell

Jet Ranger helicopter waiting for them at the San Jose Jet Center on the other side of the airport. He then gave them a ride over in his Suburban. As they rode over he explained how they would be met by another ranger at Mammoth Lake and he would serve as their guide. He said that the ranger would be able to answer any questions that they might have.

They didn't need a pilot as Sean had been flying everything from Piper Cubs to Gulfstream aircraft for about the last fifteen years and was current in most of them.

After the pre-flight on the helicopter they climbed in and Sean contacted the tower to ask for clearance which he received immediately. He took off and turned to an easterly heading climbing to about 5000 feet.

The flight took about one hour and twenty minutes and when they arrived at Mammoth Lake and got out of the helicopter they were met immediately by a lanky looking ranger from the National Park Service. He introduced himself as Rob Coleman and explained in a cheerful voice that he had been in the ranger service for about five years and had spent most of that time in the Mammoth Lake area. He gave them a summary overview of what they had noticed and in what areas. The first thing they did was take a walk along the shore of the lake.

As they walked along the ranger explained. "We've recently been getting reports from hikers."

Sean began to smell something foreign.

"What do you suppose is causing that smell," he asked Jake.

"I'm not generally sensitive to smells but that's no big surprise. You know I'm no match for your super sense but I do smell that dead fish over there," Jake said pointing to a bloated trout ahead of them on the beach.

"Yeah, we've been seeing quite a bit of that type of thing over the last week or so," explained the ranger as he walked toward the fish.

Jake said, "If I had to take a guess I'd say it looks like it was poisoned."

Sean stopped dead in his tracks. He remembered hearing those same words many years ago coming from his father about the dead fawn on the banks of the Mississippi

River. He also remembered thinking at the time that the cause may have been the pollution that was so obvious in the water however when he looked around here he saw nothing that would lead him to that conclusion. There was no apparent pollution on these shores.

"Yep, that's what we think too because otherwise the carnivores would feed on them," the ranger said.

Sean asked the ranger," Is the same thing happening to the animals?"

"We've had a few sightings of animal carcasses but very few and in all cases they've been spotted along the waters edge. The main reason we decided to report all of this to

Homeland Security is one," he paused lifting his index finger."We don't know what's causing this and we wanted to make sure that it isn't the work of some sicko trying to get back at Mother Nature. Or two," he said lifting his second finger," that it's not some natural disaster that we might somehow be able to prevent."

Sean looked from Jake to the ranger and said," I guess sabotage is always a possibility but what I'm smelling is more like sulfur. You know, like rotten eggs."

"Yeah, Now I can smell it," Jake said. "I'm pretty sure I can stop thinking about breakfast now."

"I wonder if it's coming from the water." Rob asked.

" I don't think it's coming from the water, Jake said. I think it may be coming from under the water."

The ranger thought for a moment and said," You know, these mountains are riddled with caves. If we could find one, maybe we can get under a portion of the lake and verify one way or the other if the problem is sub-terrain."

"Lead the way," Jake said to the ranger with flourish and a bow.

The ranger took them about a mile away from the lake up a narrow animal path that ascended up over a rise. Then they walked down a steep slope about five hundred feet where sure enough they located a cave.

Jake asked," Is there any chance that we could find a bear in there?" as he peered through the entrance.

"Not likely this time of year, but you wouldn't want to venture in there in November," answered the ranger seriously.

"Well," Sean said to Jake as he looked into the dark opening. "Why don't you start down into the abyss and I'll follow right behind you."

"I've got a much better idea," declared Jake. "Why don't you start down and I'll follow you! Besides, you know that according to all the girls, I'm a lot better looking than you. I'd be much harder to sacrifice." After a short pause he said, "How about we flip for it, heads you go first, tails and I'll lead the way."

"Well, ok," Sean replied skeptically.

Jake reached in his pocket, pulled out a coin and flipped it.

"It's heads," Jake announced. "After you my courageous leader." He bowed and Sean looked him quizzically. He never could figure out how Jake always seemed to win at heads or tails, but a deal was a deal and he headed down in to the cave.

Fortunately the ranger had brought along all the necessary equipment for just such an occasion.

That brings us to our present situation. Sean's stuck!

"How in the world did you get around there?" He asked Jake.

"Elementary my dear Watson," replied Jake with a smirk on his face."Back about fifteen feet there's a side tunnel that goes off to the left and goes right around this obstacle."

"That's just great. Now would you mind going back around and helping me out of here, and in case you forgot, I'm Sherlock Holmes and your Dr. Watson."

"I thought it was my turn to be Holmes."

"JACOB—".

"OK. Keep your shirt on. I'll be right there and by the way, don't go anywhere."

Jake and the ranger started to head back around. As Sean laid there stuck he felt the ground start to shake. All he could think was 'NOT NOW'. A couple of seconds later he heard the ranger yell, "Earthquake."

Fortunately it turned out to be a small tremor but it was enough to get Sean, Jake and the ranger's attention and the little bit of earth movement helped loosen up Mother Nature's grip on Sean. He started to wiggle out, then felt the strong grip of his friend's hands on his ankles. With a powerful yank, suddenly he was free.

"Thanks buddy," Sean said breathing a sigh of relief.

"No problemo, isn't that what you keep me around for," Jake replied breathing a sigh himself.

They went back to the side tunnel that Jake had discovered and took it around the place where Sean had been stuck. From there they continued on through a passageway that measured about six feet by three feet. Walking on about forty paces or so, they found themselves in a massive cavern. It had to be as big as an airplane hanger. They stood there with their mouths open gaping at the hugh stalactites hanging from the ceiling many of which came to sharp points, and the stalagmites protruding from the floor like scattered bowling pins.

In the center of the cavern there was a pond. It appeared as smooth as glass. Moving closer they detected the strong smell of sulfur and they could see by the water line on the shore that the water in the pond had been receding.

The ranger was working his way around to the other side of the pond which was about fifty feet in diameter.

"It appears that the water in this pond is coming from deep in the ground and probably being pushed up by the same seismic activity that we just felt," said Jake.

"Which probably means that this type of activity may have been going on unnoticed for many hundreds of years," continued Sean.

The ranger asked," If that's the case then why haven't we seen this type of problem before?"

"It's probably never been noticed before this because man's interest in nature's changes, be it manmade or natural, has only really come into the spotlight over the last fifty years or so and interest has intensified exponentially for about the last twenty five years."

"That makes sense considering that earthquakes occur constantly, especially around here. We're sitting right on top of both the Round Valley and the Hilton Creek fault lines. Like any other seismic activity, it's just a matter of time before the 'BIG ONE' hits," Jake said." The problem is, even though there has been an enormous amount of study on earthquakes it still remains virtually impossible to accurately predict when the 'BIG ONE' will occur."

Sean said," I think that may be exactly what has happened here. I think that maybe there was a moderately strong quake maybe twenty or thirty miles underground and it forced this water, which had picked up a lot of the natural sulfur in the ground, to be brought to the surface and mixed with the water in Mammoth Lake causing a temporary contamination of the water in the lake. Once the water recedes far enough everything should return to normal."

"Sounds logical considering the delicate ecological balance of this lake and it's surroundings," Jake replied." We'll have to run some tests on the water to confirm. I'll get some samples from this pond and the lake while you get some soil samples."

As they gathered their samples Sean heard a low rumble and called out," Guys, we've gotta go."

"What do you mean dude? I've just started collecting my samples."

"I said we gotta go and that means now. Don't you hear that? Don't you feel that?"

"What is it Sean? What do you hear?" asked Jake in a much more concerned voice.

They all looked at each other with wide eyes and at that moment it became perfectly clear what was happening. They could feel it now. Another earthquake!

"This is no small tremor," Sean yelled." I don't think this is the best place to be in a major quake. Let's get the hell out of here."

"I'll lead the way this time. Come on," Jake said as he turned on his heels and took off.

"Right behind you," Sean said.

Ranger Rob Coleman who was still on the other side of the pond started running around the pond as fast as he could. He too could feel the panic building inside of him.

As they ran they could feel the earth begin to move.

Funny thing about earthquakes, the longer they last the harder they try to kill you. It's a little like riding one of those mechanical bulls that you find in country western bars. The longer you hold on the harder it shakes and gyrates until pretty soon it either throws you on your butt or it stops. This earthquake wasn't stopping.

Just as the ranger made it around the pond the earth shook violently. He lost his balance and fell backward landing flat on his back. Sean looked back and saw Rob go down. He turned to go back and help the ranger and as he did he heard a 'CRACK'. It sounded like a gun going off. He looked up and that's when he saw the stalactite break loose from the ceiling directly above where the ranger was laying face up. Sean saw the shocked look of panic on the ranger's face as he saw what was about to happen. He was too far away to help the man and froze in his tracks as he watched in horror. The deadly point came straight down into the ranger's chest. It pinned him to the ground much like a butterfly is pinned to a collector's board. Sean knew the ranger died instantly. All he could do was stand there in shock. Suddenly he felt a tugging on his arm. It was Jake. He was yelling, "Sean, we gotta go, now. There's nothing we can do for him."

Sean snapped out of it and turned as he took off after his friend.

They ran past the spot where he had gotten stuck and continued up the incline toward the opening of the cave. As they ran around the next corner they could see the light from the opening. Then it happened. One minute they were running along and the next the floor was gone.

Jake leaped forward and as he did he reached for his pickaxe on his belt. He got it in his hand and at the last minute swung with everything he had and rammed it into the ground on the opposite side of the new fissure that had opened up. It's a good thing it stuck too because Sean who was running full bore right on his friends heels jumped at the exact same time and managed to grab Jake's legs around the knees.

Just as they slammed into the side of the fissure the earthquake stopped. Everything got eerily quiet.

Jake said," Alright Sherlock, what do we do now?"

"Elementary Dr. Watson," Sean said in his best English accent. "All I have to do is climb up your backside, get to the top and pull you to safety. In the mean time you can just lie around and wait for me to do all the heavy lifting. Oh, and by the way, do try not to let go."

At that, Sean began to do exactly what he said he would do. As he grabbed Jake by the shoulders Jake said, "In the future, remind me to flip a coin to decide who goes first." After getting to the top he then pulled Jake up and they exited the cave.

They climbed back up to the top of the hill and went back to the helicopter where Sean retrieved his satellite phone and called the National Ranger Service to report about the ranger.

Then he and Jake, exhausted and covered with dirt, sat down on a log where they shared a canteen of water and waited for the medivac chopper.

CHAPTER 2

May 6th
Mont-Tremblant, Quebec

The view was absolutely breathtaking. That was the first thing that went through her mind as she took in the panoramic view of the Laurentian Mountains.

Angelina Cartier took a moment to take all this in before she began her run. She knew that skiing downhill style at speeds of about 125km per hr she would have very little chance to enjoy the sights.

At 34 years old her sculpted features and her athletic figure looked every bit the Olympic racer she had once been. Her near perfect lightly tanned completion, auburn hair and brilliant green eyes gave her the look of a goddess. She was 5ft 7inches tall and about 119 pounds without one once of fat on her body. She had been skiing since she was 3 years old although for the last few years there hadn't had much time for it.

She began her run and quickly built up speed until soon she could feel the wind blowing through her hair. It was a feeling of total exhilaration. A feeling that she knew very few people in the world ever got the chance to experience.

As she got closer to the bottom she could see a crowd had gathered to watch her. Angelina had spent most of her adult life with people watching her and she never got used to it. It always made her feel self conscious. When she got to the bottom the crowd cheered and applauded. She could feel her face redden. While she started to kick off her skis she saw her family approach. Thank God. Her three older brothers, Jimmy, Frank, and Eddie were in front with their wives and kids. Right behind them were her mom and dad.

Her family was very close. Angelina was sure that a lot of this came from the fact that Dad was a retired sergeant from the Royal Canadian Mounties and all three of her brothers were currently in the Mounties.

She had chosen a different road which she was sure disappointed her father, although he tried not to say anything about it. She had gone to Bishop's University in Lennoxville, Quebec and studied in social sciences then on to Georgetown where she graduated at the top of her class and got a masters degree in law.

Afterward she was offered a job in law enforcement with the Federal Bureau of Investigation which she took. Because of her Canadian birth and because she was fluent in French she was stationed in Toronto, Canada and assigned to the Domestic Terror Unit for Canada which allowed her to work closely with the Canadian Mounties.

She was thrilled with the chance to work with them although her father was somewhat put out. He thought she should be working directly for the Canadian Government and not for the Americans.

She remembered him asking her at the time, "Annie, why would you want to work for them?"

"Dad, it opens a huge spectrum of opportunities."

"And the Mounties don't? He asked. "Besides, what about settling down and raising a family."

"There'll be plenty of time for that later," she replied.

That was eleven years ago. Before 9/11. Before the terrorist threat that seemed to grow like a parasite throughout the United States and Canada.

The threat was not just limited to the fanatics in the Middle East and other parts of the world. There were plenty of 'nutcases and wackos' right here on this continent. This became more and more evident after the Waco fiasco of 1993 and the tragic Oklahoma City Bombing of 1995.

Everyone became much more aware of the potential for domestic threat at that point, however nothing could possibly have had more of an impact on the entire world and especially the United States and Canada than that cowardly attack on September 11, 2001.

It was after that day that Angelina's job went from challenging to critical. She had decided that it was her job to make sure that she did everything possible to prevent anyone from doing harm to any innocent citizens of either of these two countries.

One of her main duties was to monitor the actions of the militias throughout the northwestern US and southwestern areas of Canada.

Since the 9/11 attack it had fallen on the FBI to work very closely with the Customs Departments of both countries and help keep an eye on the border between them.

As Angelina stood at the base of the ski run being congratulated by her family and other well-wishers on another spectacular performance her cell phone went off. She

reached for it immediately and after listening for a moment she hung up. She was to report back to the Hoover Building in Washington DC as soon as possible for a briefing by the director himself.

As soon as she hung up the phone she immediately kicked of her skis and headed for the lodge. Her father caught her by the arm and whispered in her ear," what is it Annie?"

"I don't know Dad but I'm supposed to leave for Washington right away for a meeting with the man himself so it must be pretty important."

His police training kicked in instantly."I'll get the car and we'll give you a ride to the airport."

CHAPTER 3

April 17th
Bend, Oregon

Chester (Chet) Ellison was born on May 9th, 1965. His parents, John and Cheryl were simple country folks. His father worked as a driver for a local dairy farm while his mother was a stay at home mom. Chester was one of three children. The oldest was his sister Ellen. She was seven years older than Chet. Then came his brother Bob who was three years younger than Ellen.

Being the youngest child, Chet was nurtured by his mother and father. It wasn't that his parents loved him any more or less than the other two children. It was just that Chet was special. He seemed to be more in touch with nature. Growing up in Bend, it was easy to see why.

Bend is nestled close to the middle of the state of Oregon in the foothills of the Deschutes National Forest. It sits on the east side of Mount St. Helens and is surrounded by beautiful forests and streams.

While Chet was growing up he spent a lot of time hiking, fishing and enjoying the great outdoors.

When he graduated from high school in 1983 he applied to and was accepted into the National Park Service as a Ranger.

He met his wife Julie in the fall of 1989 while attending a seminar on global warming in Seattle. She had grown up in Spokane, Washington in a lifestyle a lot like Chet's. Julie was a school teacher and taught in the local grammar school.

They fell in love and were married the following spring.

Three years later they had their son Daniel. The next year they had a daughter they named Alice after Chet's grandmother. Life just couldn't get any better. That was until that fateful month of April.

Chet was instructed to scout the Snake River and it's tributaries. He was told to get water samples all the way to Yellowstone. It was expected to take him about three weeks. He and his partner Andy Franklin were to leave the next day on April 18th at about 7:00am. Andy was single and unattached so as far as he was concerned this was just another way to explore the wilderness.

"Why would they send you to collect samples of the water all the way to Yellowstone?" asked Julie. "It just doesn't make any sense."

"That's why they call it government work," said Chet. "Unfortunately they never tell us why anything happens."

"Hey Julie, look at it this way," said Andy with a wide grin. "This way Chet'll have a chance to check out the area for great spots to take you and the kids this summer."

Julie just glared at him while Chet gave him one of those 'quit trying to help' looks. He and Andy continued to load their Suburban with everything they would need for what was expected to be a three week campout. He couldn't say it to Julie, but he was actually excited to be going on an adventure.

If only he knew what an adventure it would turn out to be.

Chet and Andy were ready to pull out at 6:45am the next morning. Julie had woken up when Chet got up. The kids were still asleep. She may not have been happy that her husband was leaving for three weeks but that didn't change the fact that she loved him and would miss him. As she waved goodbye to him she had a strange feeling in her gut. It was almost like a premonition. She didn't know why but she was sure that something bad was going to happen. It was so strong that she almost ran after the car to stop Chet from going. Instead she watched as the Suburban disappeared around the corner of their tree lined street. Only then did she turn and head back into the house to begin her day of caring for the children.

They headed north on highway 97 to the Columbia River, then east on highway 84 following the river to where it turned north into the state of Washington. They took highway 395 north to Richland and Kennewick. Not only is this the area where the Snake River Tributary comes off the Columbia, it's also where the only active nuclear power plant in the state of Washington is located.

"It's hard to believe that they actually built a nuclear reactor on the Columbia River," said Chet as they passed the sign for the turn off to the US Department of Energy Hanford Site.

"Yeah," said Andy." But you have to remember that in1943 when this plant was built America was at war and there was a very real threat that Germany would beat us in the race to create the nuclear bomb. They must have figured that this location was isolated enough to prevent anyone from suspecting that they were producing plutonium that would be used in the Manhattan Project. I read that they sent it to Los Alamos, New Mexico and it was that plutonium that was used to create 'The Fat Man Bomb' used in Nagasaki, Japan. It helped stop the Second World War."

"I guess so but to put it here on the banks of one of the most beautiful rivers in the world just seems wrong."

"They probably chose this location because they figured that a nuclear reactor would need an enormous amount of water to cool the fuel rods," said Andy.

They made a turn and started up the Snake River. For most of the way they had good road and made pretty good time. The department had provided them with the essential testing equipment which included 30 test jars with labels to mark each sample with the proper GPS coordinates. They figured the river was about 1000 miles long so one sample every 50 miles or so would do it. They were also equipped with a satellite cell phone.

They made it to their fourth test sight when they decided to set up camp for the night.

They were about 50 miles from Lewiston, Idaho.

It was pretty desolate where they were and that made it just that much more enjoyable. This is why Chet had signed up for the rangers.

While they were setting up camp Andy said," the only reason that I can figure that they sent us out here to collect these samples is they must think that there is some kind of contamination happening here.

"Maybe, but I can't imagine anyone being that insensitive to the environment and allowing that kind of thing to happen. Not with the way everyone has become so environmentally conscious."

"It is possible that if we are right and there is something wrong with the water it could be some kind of natural occurrence."

"It's possible but it makes me wonder why they haven't told us anything about what's going on," replied Chet as he leaned on the tailgate of the Suburban.

"Maybe they don't know themselves. Maybe they're just on a fishing expedition."

"Correction, maybe they're just sending us on a fishing expedition."

With all this talk about fishing they decided to try their luck fishing for their dinner. They each had brought their fishing gear so they grabbed their poles and walked down to the river. In this desolate area of the river it didn't take long and they both of them began to get bites. They actually were enjoying themselves and soon each had caught their second fish. They decided that was plenty for dinner but they were having so much fun that it was decided they would continue fishing using the catch and release method. After about a half hour of this it was just about time to gather their gear and head back to camp when they were joined by a large male grizzly bear. He had come out of the trees across the river and began to wade out into the river to see if he could catch his dinner too.

Chet and Andy had both been in the rangers long enough to know that as long as you didn't invade his domain he would not consider you a threat and thus he would leave you alone. The only problem was that this bear evidently hadn't read the ranger handbook on grizzly bear behavior in the wild. Instead of just fishing on his side of the river he kept swimming toward their side.

Andy said." You know Chet? It sure looks like that bear is planning on getting his dinner from this side of the river."

"It sure does. And from the look in his eyes I'd say that fish is not what he has in mind for the main entrée. I think it might be a real good idea to get our stuff together and head back to camp.

"Sounds good to me," said Andy as he began quickly gathering his gear while keeping one eye on the approaching bear.

"I'll go ahead and leave one of my fish here on the bank of the river. He might just be after our catch figuring it would be easier than catching his own. Maybe that'll be enough to satisfy him."

By this time the bear was about halfway across the river and still coming on strong.

His menacing eyes were still fixed on them.

With the rest of the fish and their gear they began backing away from the river and heading back to their camp. When they got back they immediately took out their hunting rifles from the Suburban and loaded them. Each gun was a Ruger M77 Mark11 in 308 which is considered one of the best weapons for large game including bears. Chet thought about grabbing his 9 millimeter Glock but decided against it knowing that if you try to shoot a large grizzly bear with a relatively small caliber pistol all you'll manage to do is make him real mad. There had even been reports of people who had shot a grizzly in the head with a pistol and the bullet had bounced off and if that happens all you have left is one really pissed off bear.

"You know Chet, the last place I expected to need a rifle was fishing the Snake River but I'm sure glade we have them with us. I just hope that bear stays down by the river so I don't have to use it."

"I hope so too," replied Chet. "You know I think it might be a real good idea to put some distance between us and that grizzly."

They decided to move their camp down the river. They packed up their stuff as fast as they could always keeping their weapons within an arm's length and always keeping a sharp eye out for the 1500 pound animal. It was a hassle to move camp but they figured it just wouldn't be right for a couple of rangers to have to kill a grizzly bear just because they were too lazy to move.

The two of them drove down the road about 5 miles until they were pretty sure they were far enough away from the bear encounter. They set up camp again and built a fire to cook the fish. After they finished cleaning up the camp they sat down in front of the fire.

Andy said." What do you suppose got into that bear?"

"I don't know but that sure wasn't normal behavior. Even for a grizzly. It was as if he thought that we were acting aggressively and reacted instinctively the only way he knew how."

"I sure wouldn't want to see him react that way with a family that was out here camping. They might not have the sense to react quickly enough to get away."

Chet said," that's true. And the average family out for a camping trip wouldn't be armed with high powered hunting rifles. The most these campers come armed with is a cell phone and a camera. I think that tomorrow when we reach the National Park Service in Lewiston we better let them know what happened so they can send out a team to check it out."

"Good idea, and don't let me forget to find out who the local shipping agent is for these water samples. I guess they're supposed to be sent to the Center for Decease Control in Atlanta." After a moments thought Andy added," I wonder what's really going on out here."

Chet was also trying to figure out what it was that they had got themselves into when he said, "Well, I'm sure we'll find out soon enough. For now we better get some sleep if we're gonna get an early start tomorrow."

The next morning they were in their car by seven and continued following the river which took them into Lewiston, Idaho. On the way there they stopped once to get another water sample. They now had five samples to be sent out to the CDC.

They stopped in at the National Park Service Visiting Center to check in and report the incident with the grizzly bear to the center's senior ranger. His name was Jack

Mathews. They talked about it for a while and Ranger Mathews said he would take another ranger who was experienced in tracking with him up river to the same area and see if they could locate the aggressive bear.

When they finished discussing the bear they asked about shipping their water samples. They were told that there was a local UPS store that was used by the Ranger Service just up the street and they were given directions to it.

While they were getting their instructions Chet and Andy ask Ranger Mathews if he had any idea what was going on with the water. The ranger said he hadn't heard of any problems however he seemed to have a hard time looking the rangers in the eye directly.

As they started out the door Chet turned to the ranger and asked," You know, it's just about 10:00 o'clock and I'm starting to get pretty hungry. I don't suppose you'd like to show us where we might get some breakfast. I'm buying."

"Sounds like a great idea to me," he replied never wanting to seem inhospitable or miss out on a free meal. "There's a real nice little coffee shop right across from the UPS store, serves a real fine breakfast. Why don't you two follow me over?"

"We'll be right behind you," said Andy who would never turn down a meal.

They followed the ranger for about a quarter mile down the road where he pulled up in front of a cute little restaurant called Debbie's. The three of them went inside and headed for a table towards the back of the café. As they were heading to the table they passed a nice looking waitress in a pink service dress with an apron. She looked up and smiled," How you doing Jack? You want your regular?"

"Yes please Deb and would you mind giving my friends here a menu?"

"You got it," she replied eyeing the strangers.

They got to their table and sat down taking the menus from the waitress. She brought each of them coffee and as soon as she was out of ear shot Chet asked," Jack, I was hoping you could shed a little light on what's going on around here and why they've got Andy and me out getting water samples along the Snake River?"

Jack stared at both of them then looked down at his cup of coffee. "I'm not exactly sure how to answer that." He leaned forward and waited for Debbie who had come back to the table to take their orders. When she was done and had walked away he said quietly," About a week ago we were out doing our normal rounds and we came across a couple camping by the river. At least they had started out camping," He looked around to make sure that no one else was listening, then continued," It looked like they had been there about a week. Guys I don't know what happened to them but someone or something had attacked them. They were both dead. It looked like it had happened that morning or possibly during the night."

Andy looked at Chet and said," That's terrible. Do you have any idea what happened to them?"

"Not really. We're still waiting for an autopsy."

"It may have been an animal attack," replied Chet. "Something like that is extremely rare but certainly not unheard of."

"I know but it wasn't just the attack that got our attention. Judging by their gear and the way they went about camping these two were not amateurs. They had done a solid job of securing their camp sight. They even hung their coolers and food products in the trees. Everything considered they were pretty careful. They even had mace with them but hadn't used it." Jack thought for a moment as he had a sip of his coffee. "It was the other things they had done that really puzzled us. They had dug fox holes. Fox holes just like the military. Holes in the ground. It was as though they knew something was after them. And not just that, they had rigged bobby traps all around their camp. After what you two told me about the grizzly and how strange it was behaving it kind of got me thinking again that maybe that bear had been the attacker. The only trouble with that theory is we only found tracks from much smaller animals like wolves or even coyotes."

"Wait a minute," said Andy in disbelief. "You're saying that you think a pack of wolves or coyotes attacked an experienced couple at a camp spot?"

"That's what I'm saying. They had been savagely killed but not eaten. It was as though the attacker had rabies or something but there haven't been any reports of rabies in these parts for many years and I don't think I've ever heard of a grizzly bear with rabies. And it still doesn't explain the weird behavior of the campers. Strangest thing I've ever seen." The ranger waited as Debbie came back with their orders.

When she walked away Chet said," So the people in Washington DC must think that there may be a problem with the water and that it may have contributed or caused the unusual behavior."

"That would be my guess," said Jack.

Andy stopped devouring his breakfast, sat back and said," Well at least that gives us something to go on."

"That's a fact," said Chet. "I'll tell you what Jack. We'll keep our eyes open for anything strange or unusual on up the river and if we see anything we'll call you right away."

"Thanks guys. I'll take any information I can get. It goes without saying I'm pretty stumped on this."

They finished their meal, Chet paid the bill and left a 20% tip for Debbie. They walked out the restaurant and out front exchanged phone numbers with the promise to report anything unusual.

Chet and Andy got into their Suburban and headed south through the town to continue their assignment of collecting water samples up the Snake River.

They were traveling south now which is where the river becomes the Oregon-Idaho border. About one hundred miles from Lewiston is the area called Hells Canyon. It's the deepest gorge in the United States and provides breathtaking views for about fifty miles or so.

The only problem with Hells Canyon is there are only three roads that go through the mountains to access the river. The only way Chet and Andy were able to follow the river was to drive on a fire trail road that runs along the gorge.

Andy was driving and the going was very slow. He began to speed up a little in hopes to get through the canyon by nightfall.

"You might want to slow down a bit Andy," commented Chet as was lookingnervously out his side window at the shear drop down about one hundred feet to the river below. "I promised Julie I'd make it home in one piece."

"No worries buddy. I used to drive in dirt track races before I became a ranger. This is a piece of cake."

Andy had no sooner finished his sentence when up ahead there was a tight left turn. As he started into the turn they both could feel the back of the Suburban begin to slide.

Even though the car was in four wheel drive the combination of the vehicle's momentum and the powdery dirt on the road made the turn very treacherous. Andy corrected perfectly as they came out of the turn and just as they started to relax they saw three elk on the road in front of them. Andy turned the wheel to the right just in time and as they screamed past the elk the front wheel of the truck left the road. The rest was all gravity.

The Suburban tilted forward and to the right and began to roll off the road.

Andy yelled," Hold on! We're going over."

He wasn't telling Chet anything that he didn't already know. He could tell because at that moment he was looking straight out the side window and down at the river below. He was suddenly struck by the absolute fear that he would never see his wife or children ever again. It was like it was happening in slow motion. The rear tire went over the edge and suddenly they were rolling over and over down the steep cliff. As the airbags deployed all he could think about was to hold on tight. He felt like this is what must feel like to be in a cement mixer and he was the concrete. It all seemed so violent and he was sure that there was only one thing that would stop it and that wouldn't be good. As they rolled over and over he felt a wave of nausea hit him but things were happening too fast now to think about it. He looked to his left and saw Andy holding on to the steering wheel with a look of horror on his face. Everything in the vehicle was flying everywhere including the glass test jars which were obviously shattered because he could see and feel the small shards of glass flying around the inside of the truck and cutting into his face and arms.

Suddenly he saw Andy's door fly open. It broke off and was gone. They continued to spin completely out of control. Just when Chet thought he couldn't stand the noise anymore the sound stopped. They were still spinning just as fast as they were before but everything was completely quiet. They had rolled down the steep incline of the mountain and off the shear cliff that made up the river's gorge. They were now airborne and tumbling in a free fall to the fast moving rapids of the Snake River.

Then came the impact. It felt like they had hit a brick wall. The car landed upside down. Chet blacked out and when he came to he saw that his seatbelt had held and he was suspended from the seat upside down. He was sure that his shoulder was broken and he instantly saw the water rushing into the vehicle. It was floating down the river but it was obvious that it was going to sink and pretty soon. He was still having trouble figuring out how he was still alive. He looked over to check on Andy and was shocked to see the driver seat empty. Andy was gone. He must have gotten ejected when his door was torn off.

The water was now coming in at an alarming rate and Chet started fumbling with his seatbelt trying to release it. After a short moment of panic the button released and he dropped on his head to what was now the inverted ceiling. While he was trying to get out of the seatbelt the car rolled and the open driver's door went under water. The freezing water immediately flooded into the interior of the car. He was trapped. He still had a pocket of air on his side but the car was rapidly filling with water as it slammed into the rocks that made up the class four rapids. His broken shoulder was being hammered constantly and with each impact a white hot searing pain shot through his body. He reached down to open his door. It was jammed tight from all the pounding it had taken. Then he tried to roll down the window but immediately remembered they were electric. By this time he knew he was in trouble. As the water continued to rise and the car continued to be bounced around it was getting so he could not keep his head above the water level. He kept swallowing large amounts of water and it was making him cough violently to the point of gagging. As he became more and more desperate to find a way out his vision began to blur and the area around his vision was starting to cloud. He knew that if he didn't do something right now he was done for. For lack of any other choice and as a last ditch effort he took a deep breath, leaned back and with both his feet together kicked at the front wind shield with every ounce of strength he had left. Nothing happened. He tried again and this time he thought he felt it give a little. He leaned back and gave it a third try. This time the corner of the window came loose. With renewed hope he kicked again and again. It finally came loose. He swam out through the opening his lungs were on fire and as he went for the surface he was sure that he was going to loose consciousness. Suddenly he broke the surface and he could see the sky. The beautiful blue ski and he could breath. Then just as suddenly he realized he was in the middle of the class four rapids.

The river was heaving all around him. It was like being in the middle of the Atlantic Ocean during a storm. With his damaged shoulder he was completely at the mercy of the raging current. Soon the water was rolling and thrashing him. It was completely disorienting and he had absolutely no control. A massive wave hit him from the side and literally drove him directly into a huge boulder. He tried to protect his head from the impact but the river was too strong and he hit hard. As he did his hand fell limp from the large rock and everything around him went dark.

CHAPTER 4

May 7th
Washington DC

Angelina was in a yellow cab pulling up to the Hoover Building. When the cab came to a stop she gave the driver two twenty dollar bills and told him to keep the change. He was obviously from the middle east and took the money without acknowledging her which irritated her. *(you'd think that a thirty percent tip would at least warrant a simple thank you. Rude, rude, rude.)*

She hopped out of the cab and walked quickly to the front door checking her watch as she went in. It was 9:00am sharp. When she entered the building she was immediately greeted by a good looking young man who looked up from a folder in front of him. He was obviously in excellent physical condition and he smiled at her flashing his perfect set of teeth. He was wearing a perfectly pressed non-descript grey suit with a white shirt, a blue tie and was sitting at a well polished non-descript brown walnut desk.

It had been a couple of years since Angelina had been in this building.

"May I help you," he asked in a voice that was much too cheery for this early in the morning.

"Yes please," she replied while she reached into her purse for her badge and identification. "I'm agent Angelina Cartier of the Toronto office. I'm here to see the director at his request. I believe he's expecting me."

He looked her up and down as though he was checking to see what the difference was between Canadian women and American women and said," If you'll have a seat I'll call the director's office and let them know you're here.

Angelina smiled and sat down on one of the leather chairs in the lobby.

It wasn't long before she heard the familiar ding of the elevator and a man stepped out and walk up to her. Michele did a double take of the man and chuckled to herself. The man coming toward her could have been a clone to the man behind the desk except his tie was red. Obviously a power color. She couldn't help but wonder to herself if all of the agents on the top floor wore red ties.

"Good morning Agent Cartier," he said as he held out a hand and smiled. "I'm agent Allen Carroll, the director's assistant."

"Good morning," Angelina replied taking his hand and returning his smile.

"The director is expecting you so I'm here to escort you on up. If you'll come this way," he said as he gestured with his hand toward the elevators.

Angelina knew that until you were cleared and received a pass you had to be escorted while in the building. After 9/11 no one was taking any chances. That rule she knew held true for most of the official buildings in Washington.

They entered the elevator and Agent Carroll used his identification card for the scanner and pressed the button for the top floor. When the doors opened they were greeted by another agent who was also seated at a desk facing the elevator. He smiled and Agent Carroll nodded to him. He acknowledged the agent and stared at Angelina while his right hand stayed down and out of sight. He was obviously holding a gun under the desk and never took his eyes off of them until they had passed him and gone through the double glass doors on the opposite side of the entryway.

Angelina couldn't help but notice the lavish decorations and plush carpet that adorned both the entry and the rest of the area. She saw Ansell Adams stills showing Yosemite's Halfdome and many others including a Monet print, or was it a print?

There was soft background music playing as they passed four desks. Three of them were occupied by people busy doing what people did in the office of the Director of the Federal Bureau of Investigation. Until this moment Angelina had been pretty calm about this meeting but just being here in this office made her stomach tighten.

As they walked past an empty desk that she assumed was Agent Carroll's they approached a set of double mahogany doors with a brass placard on the door that read,

OFFICE OF JONATHAN MASON
DIRECTOR
FEDERAL BUREAU OF INVESTIGATION

Agent Carroll knocked lightly on the door and from the other side they heard a deep voice say "Come in."

They entered and Carroll said, "Mr. Director this is Agent Angelina Cartier of the Toronto office."

The director looked up from a file he was reading, closed it and set it down on his desk in front of him. He stood up and walked around his desk extending his hand. Angelina shook his hand and he said," Agent Cartier, It's so good of you to make the trip on such short notice."

He said this like she had a choice. "Thank you for having me sir." As soon as she said it she thought,(*boy did that sound stupid*).

Director Mason was large in both height and girth. She estimated he was about 6'4" and probably weighed in at about 260 pounds. He had probably played football as a young man and he carried himself quite well for as big as he was. He looked to be in his 50's and his voice seemed to boom even when he was talking normally.

"I'm sure you're curious about why we asked you to come in so I'll get right to the point." He said this as he moved to a pair of leather captain's chair and motioned for Angelina to take a seat. "We've been getting a lot of suspicious chatter over the airwaves recently. That leads us to believe that there may be something being planned by the bad guys and whatever it is it's got the people over at the NSA worried and when the NSA gets worried the White House gets worried and then I get a call from the president's national security adviser and well, you can see where I'm going with this. The NSA is constantly monitoring the airwaves for specific words or phrases that could be linked to possible terrorist activity. Once it gets something it pays close attention to that area and begins to assess any potential threat to national security. That's where we get involved. Do you follow me so far?"

Angelina nodded and said," Yes sir, but can I ask how this involves me? Is this potential threat coming from the Toronto area?"

"No it's not. The area we're referring to is the northwestern section of the United States. Specifically from the Yellowstone, Wyoming area west to the Pacific Ocean including the states between and north into British Columbia then east through Alberta and parts of Saskatchewan. With your connections to the Canadian Mounties and the fact that you've been working with them for quite a while you became the logical choice for this assignment."

"I'm flattered that you chose me," Angelina said with a somewhat puzzled look on her face. "But that's an awfully large area to cover. What exactly am I looking for?"

"We believe that what we're hearing may be coming from one or more of the local militias. That area is crawling with every group of nutcases from the Arian Nation to the National Coalition for Personal Rights, including everything in between. These are some really nasty folks. Whatever it is that their planning, it can't be good. We need you to go up there and snoop around. Shake the trees and see what falls out. It goes without saying that you'll have to be very careful. We need to find out what their up to but don't forget Agent Cartier that these people can be very dangerous."

Angelina was in shock as she thought of the scope of what the director was asking her to do. "I'm not sure where to begin sir. Am I going up there alone?"

The director got up and walked over to the office door. He opened it and said," Al, would you bring in the file on the northwest situation please?" He closed the door and came back to his seat.

Agent Carroll came in almost immediately carrying a rather large file and crossed the room to hand it to Director Mason.

"Thank you Al." He took the file and without opening it handed it to Angelina. "This is information we've collected on as many of the militias as we could find. You'll also find transcripts of many of the intercepted cell phone conversations that we've been able to gather. The Patriot Act allows us to gather information when we feel it's vital to the security of the United States or if we feel that there is a potential terrorist threat. In this case we feel there is enough to warrant an investigation. There are many splinter groups and many members of these militias. Even though there are some of them that are not dangerous to our country, a lot of them are. We also don't want to alert them. We want to stop them!"

Angelina looked down at the thick folder. The cover read "NORTHWEST MILITIAS"

Mason went on," I want you to keep a low profile and go in undercover. There is a two man team from the Department of Homeland Security that is set to fly out of Andrews tomorrow. Their looking for some kind of problem with the water systems in that area and I want you to join them. You'll have credentials showing your name and that you are from the Center of Disease Control. They, of course will know that you're actually with the FBI but they'll be the only ones including the local law enforcement.

We're pretty sure that many of the local police are either members of the militias or are sympathetic to their cause. If you get into trouble and need help you'll have to contact one of the local FBI offices. They will assist you any way they can. Any questions?"

Angelina sat there for a moment. Her mind was spinning. (*Any questions. only about a million*). She sat back and was about to ask where she should begin when the director said," If you're ready to get started I'll have Agent Carroll direct you to a temporary office where you can begin studying the file." He stood obviously indicating that the meeting was over. "Unfortunately because of the sensitive nature of this investigation that file will have to stay in this building. Take all of the time you need. You're booked on a Homeland Security Citation CJ1 jet scheduled to fly out tomorrow at 10:00am."

He walked back over to his desk and picking up the file he had originally been reading he said," Before you go you might also want to take this file with you and familiarize yourself with your two traveling companions. What information we have on them is in there." He handed her the folder. "I think you'll find it quite interesting."

At that he sat back in his chair. "I think that just about wraps it up. Good luck with the assignment and don't forget to keep your head down and your eyes peeled. We'll expect daily reports and above all be careful.

"I'll do my best sir," Angelina replied understanding that the meeting was over. She stood and walked out the door where Agent Carroll was waiting for her.

She was taken down one floor and led down the hall to a non-descript office where the agent gave her a new ID badge which would allow her to move around the building freely. He also left his card and told her that if she needed anything to call him directly using the number on the card.

She walked into the office and was glad to see that it had a metal desk with a chair, two chairs facing the desk and on the credenza next to the side wall was a coffee pot with a full pot of fresh coffee and a couple of coffee mugs. Thank God for small favors.

The desk was clear with the exception of a telephone and a desk pad.

Michele laid the two folders on the desk and went for the coffee. She sat down and opened the top folder which contained the cell phone transcripts and the information on the different militia groups. The names were all different but they were all basically the same. They all seemed to hate the government yet they all loved their country. Some of them, like the Arian Nation, were racial extremists that could only be rivaled by such groups as the KKK. The one thing they all seemed to share was the mindset that no matter what the government did it was wrong.

One of the groups seemed to stand out from the rest. They called themselves The Keepers. They spent a tremendous amount of their time and resources sending out hate mail depicting the government as the great polluters of our country. They were specific when they explained about allowing the forests to be clear cut, and allowing the American Indians to net as many Salmon as they pleased not just for their consumption but to sell to the general public with no regard for the environment. They wrote about allowing large conglomerates to build and operate nuclear power plants in locations that when they failed, which was explained in their correspondence as inevitable, would do horrific and irreparable damage. How they were letting companies continue to create new chemicals and cleaners that were so potent that if mixed together could create extremely dangerous and toxic waste. The list went on and on.

Their answers to all of these offences were to band together and attack the government with violence if necessary.

Angelina sat back and thought about that. Could a group like The Keepers act on such a threat? Where would they get the financial backing? Where would they get the weapons necessary to actually make a stand against the United States Government?

The answer came as she read the FBI summary on the next page. This group was for real. Their financial worth was in the millions. The money was being donated by thousands of contributors spread out all across the country and a large portion of it was being sent from Canada. According to the report, they had several camps spread throughout the northwest and the Canadian southwest.

According to the FBI file it said that it was believed that The Keepers had stockpiles of weapons at several of their camps. They had everything from M-16 rifles and grenade launchers to C4 plastic explosives and shoulder held missile launchers.

This was just one of the potentially dangerous groups. All she could think was how in the world she was going to find any of these groups, let alone infiltrate them and determine which of them posed a real threat. It sounded like they all did.

She set the folder aside and picked up the file containing the information on the two people she'd be traveling with. She opened it and began reading. The first paragraph explained that they were both engineers. One was a chemical engineer while the other was a hydro engineer, (*whatever that was*). Oh, that's just great. Here she was being sent out to find some of the most dangerous people in the western hemisphere with a couple of Ivy League geeks.

She sighed and got up to get another cup of coffee. She brought it back to the desk, sat down and continued reading.

As she read the report she began to get a different impression of these two guys. They had been going out in the field together on many different assignments since they had been brought into Homeland Security after 9/11. Their travels took them on some very unusual "adventures." The more Angelina read the more the report sounded like something out of a dime store novel.

They had been sent into some pretty rough places including the everglades of southern Florida to check out an oil spill that was affecting some of the wildlife including alligators which it appeared that they had a couple of run ins with.

On one assignment they had gone into the Alabama/Georgia Bayous to try to find out what was contaminating the water and affecting the water moccasin population. It had turned out to be Moon shiners dumping their waste into the water system. That had turned into some kind of a gun battle. And then there was their trip to Mammoth Lake.

These two started to sound like something out of an Indiana Jones' Raiders of the Lost Ark movie.

(Well,) Angelina thought. *(They obviously have been very lucky in the past but their not trained agents from the FBI).* She knew that where they were going it was going to take a lot more than just luck to get the answers they needed without getting their heads blown off. If these two geeks thought that she was going to nursemaid them through this assignment they were in for a very big disappointment.

She got herself another cup of coffee and spent the rest of the day pouring over the information about the different militia groups and at 6:00 o'clock she decided she had read enough to understand the basic mindset of these people. She sat there pressing the palms of her hands to her temples as she tried to think of the best way to approach this. She decided there was no way she was going to figure out a way tonight and decided she'd have to try to formulate a plan on the plane tomorrow. She got up from the desk, gathered up the files and left the office headed upstairs to Agent Carroll's office where she found him still at his desk.

"Well hello there. I assume you have everything committed to memory," he said with a congenial smile.

"Not quite," she replied as she laid the two files on his desk. "But I do think I have enough to begin."

"Very good, I've taken the liberty of booking you into the Hay-Adams Hotel for this evening and I've arranged for a ride. He's downstairs at the basement level. He knows who you are and I'll call him and have him meet you at the elevators."

With that he turned back to his computer screen which was obviously the signal that the conversation was over. Angelina smiled at his back and walked away to the elevators.

When she got off the elevator at the parking garage level she was met by another clone, this one had a green tie on and Angelina smiled to herself.

"If you'll follow me Agent Cartier the car is right over here," he said as he took her overnight bag and gestured to a black Lincoln limousine parked about twenty feet away. "By the way," he said with a smile. "My name is Hank. Agent Hank Meyer. Please call me Hank."

"It's nice to meet you Hank," She replied. "You can call me Annie."

(*Now this is more like it*), Annie thought as she followed the driver to the car.

The ride was very short. She took in the sights while they made their way to the hotel past the capitol building and the white house.

When they pulled up to the hotel Hank came around and opened the door.

"I'm sure you'll be happy with this hotel," He said. "I'll be back in the morning to take you to the airport at 8:30am. I hope you enjoy your evening."

Annie turned on her heels and headed for the registration desk. After checking in she was escorted to her room by a bellman who she tipped five dollars.

The room was unbelievable. She made a b-line for the shower tearing her clothes off as she went. When she was done showering she filled the soaking tub with the hottest water she could handle using a generous amount of the bath oils that the hotel provided and settled into the hot steaming water to soak all the days tensions away.

When she had finished drying her hair she laid down on the bed and drifted off to sleep. She awoke up at 10:00pm and realized she was starving. She ordered a Steak Sandwich from room service along with a house salad with bleu cheese dressing and an ice cold Dos Equis beer.

When it arrived she signed the check and the server left the room. As soon as the door was closed she all but ran to the small dining table where the server had set up the dinner.

She was ravaged and began eating the sandwich and french fries with gusto. Every few bites she set the sandwich down and had a couple of forks full of salad. In what seemed like minutes the food was gone. She sat back and sipped the beer while she thought about what the next day would bring.

Normally she might even be a little excited about traveling with two male companions, but the thought of the two scientists left her feeling apprehensive about this trip. She thought about it and decided there wasn't much she could do about it.

She checked her bags and was glad to see that she had a lot of her foul weather gear with her after the ski trip. She was pretty sure that she was going to need it.

Michele finished the beer and called the front desk and asked for a wakeup call for 7:00am and asked for some coffee and breakfast to be brought to the room at 7:30.

She pulled back the covers on the bed, got in and laid her head back on the pillow. It felt like she was on a cloud and she immediately fell sound asleep.

CHAPTER 5

April 20ˢᵗ
Hells Canyon
Snake River, Idaho

Chet slowly opened his eyes to find himself lying face down on a rock the size of a small car. He was having some trouble getting his left eye open. He reached up with his left hand and felt where his eye should have been. Instead he discovered a lump the size of his fist and as he touched it he felt a searing pain that made his eyes water. The swelling had completely closed his eye. Then he tried to push himself up to a kneeling position but he found that his right arm would not work. Had he lost it? He carefully reached for it with his left hand to check and was relieved to find it still there but when he moved it he received what felt like a jolt of lightning that shot through his body making him scream in agony.

He managed to roll himself over onto his back which was no easy task because he had to push with his left hand and use his legs to gain enough leverage. The move caused him to roll over his injured arm. The pain was like none he had ever experienced and almost caused him to pass out.

He laid there on his back and began to look around at his surroundings. He was on the bank of a fast moving river. His clothes were torn and damp. (*I must have pulled myself out of the river. But how did I get in the river?*) As he thought about it he started to panic. (*Where am I and how long have I been here?*) Then his throat tightened as it dawned on him, (*Who am I?*) No matter how hard he tried he could not remember his name.

He hadn't been wearing his uniform. The Suburban had sunk to the bottom of the river. He had obviously hit his head hard and judging by the lump above eye he was pretty sure he had a concussion. His shoulder hurt so bad that he thought that it might be broken and all he could think about was 'What the hell happened'!

He couldn't even remember how long he'd been there. All he knew was that he was dam cold and starving. Judging by the position of the sun he figured it must be morning. He sat up and started to struggle to his feet and the world around him started spinning. As he passed out he fell back to the ground. Fortunately he landed off the rock in an area that was full of soft dirt and pine needles.

When he woke the next time the sun was high over his head. He could feel the warmth spreading over his entire body. His clothes were almost dry. He gently began to sit up, this time moving very slowly. Again he checked his surroundings but could not remember anything about the events that brought him to this place.

He got himself to his feet and slowly made his way to the river's edge where he bent down and cupped his hand to get himself a drink of water. His mouth was dry and he had what felt like an unquenchable thirst. As he drank hand after hand of water he kept trying

to figure out what had happened but the more he tried to remember the more his head hurt. The only thing he could think about was how hungry he was.

He checked his pockets and the only thing he found was a small folding knife. (*Great*), he thought. (*A lot of good this will do me*). As he said that he looked down at the water and saw a pair of rainbow trout swim past him and once they had passed him they entered a small pool of relatively calm water to sun themselves.

Suddenly he had an idea. He stood and gingerly walked over the rocks and up to the tree line where he began looking around. He found a branch that had fallen. It was about an inch around, about 6 feet long and pretty straight. He held it in the center and pulled his arm back as if to throw it like a spear. (*This should do it*), he thought. He sat down on a rock and took out his knife. He began whittling at the end of the shaft and soon he had it cut to a sharp point. He held it up and checked it out. (*Not bad for a rookie*), he boasted.

He made his way back down to the river and approached the same pool that the fish had been in and was pleased to find them still there only now there were four of them. He inched his way closer to the edge so that he was now looking almost straight down into the water. He slowly raised his new weapon and froze. He was sure the fish were watching him so he waited until he was sure the fish weren't looking. Then he struck!

He missed. He was sure that it was because he wasn't use to the spear. Also he was right handed and because of his injury was having to use his left hand which made it a lot harder to throw accurately. He recovered his spear and tried again and again he missed. This went on for about a half an hour. He decided that catching fish this way was a lot harder than it looked. He was beginning to get very tired and was thinking about giving up but he knew he had to keep trying. He felt like he was starving.

He chose to give it one more try. This time his aim was true. Before the fish could wiggle itself free he flipped it up onto the bank. He hurried over to the fish as it flopped around frantically and hit it with a rock. He sat down and pulled out his pocket knife. He began cutting off pieces of meat from his catch and eating it raw. If anyone had been watching they would have been sickened by the ferociousness with witch he attacked the meal. He ate as though he was afraid someone might come along and take it away from him.

When he had ate enough of it he went back to the water and put his head down and drank directly from the river. It was as though he couldn't get enough water fast enough. He ignored the fact the water (which was crystal clear) tasted a little off. He couldn't place the taste but it wasn't normal. It didn't matter. He was thirsty!

Exhausted and full he made his way back up to the tree line were he found a patch of soft mulch and proceeded to lay down and fall fast asleep.

The next time he woke it was just beginning to get light. He had obviously slept all the way through the night. His eye felt as though the swelling had gone down some. He tried to move his arm and was surprised to find that he could move it a little although to do so caused him quite a bit of pain. (*At leased it's not broken*), he thought gratefully.

He stood and looked around. He still couldn't remember a thing. The only thing he knew was that he was extremely thirsty. After having another long drink from the river he decided he couldn't stay here.

He decided to head upriver. He didn't know why. He just felt that that was the direction he should go. He grabbed his homemade spear and started walking.

After about two hours of walking through the trees he began to get hungry again. A half an hour later he was starving. He made his way back down to the water and began to try his skill with the spear again. This time he had much better luck and within fifteen minutes he had caught one. It's a good thing too because by then he was starving again. His approach to eating the fish was a replay of the afternoon before and when he was done he had developed a thirst that was almost unquenchable.

He drank from the river for several minutes before he was ready to continue his walking. He returned to the tree line where it was easier to walk and continued heading up river. He didn't know where he was going or what he was supposed to do when he got there but he was sure that the answers were up river.

Chet continued walking up river for the next two days. By this time the swelling above his left eye was almost gone and he found that he was able to use his right arm almost without pain.

He'd walk during the days catching and eating the raw fish and drinking the cool water directly from the river.

He still had no recollection of who he was or what had happened to put him into this situation. The only thing he could think about was survival.

At night he was able to find a downed tree or a hollowed out tree stump that allowed him to take a little refuge from the cold night air. He thought about trying to make a fire to cook the fish but every time he decided to try and build one the pangs of hunger seemed to take over him and by the time he actually caught his dinner he was so famished that it distorted his thoughts and he forgot all about cooking. All he could think about was eating that fish!

On the third day it was just about dusk when he felt the need for nourishment and walked down to the river to get some dinner. It was getting a little harder to see because of the lack of daylight and it took him much longer to get his catch. By the time he got one he was crazed with hunger and tore into his dinner with a lot more gusto than normal. As he was tearing into the fish he looked up to find himself starring into the eyes of a grey wolf. It was about the size of a good size German Sheppard.

It was about ten feet away from him and by the way it was looking at him and his catch it was obvious that the animal was just as hungry as he was. He slowly looked around to find his spear slightly behind him and to his left. As he carefully reached for it the wolf began a low menacing growl lowering his head and bearing his teeth. Chet felt no fear and he also began to growl as he picked up his spear and began to get to his feet. He looked at the wolf and all he could think about was MEAT!

The wolf must have sensed what he was thinking because instead of charging it began to solely move back. As it did Chet moved forward and just as the wolf was getting ready to bolt Chet pounced. The wolf yelped as Chet came down with his spear into the back of the animal. He stabbed again and again with the fury of a wild animal. Within seconds the wolf was dead and Chet stood over him panting. He brought the spear over his head and howled like a beast.

For two more days he continued up the river. Nothing had changed as far as his memory but his thirst continued. He was also feeling more and more paranoid. He didn't know how long he had been out here but he thought it was probably about a week.

He also didn't know how far he had walked but it seemed like forever. He had actually made it about forty miles. He didn't know it but he was coming to the end of Hells Canyon and was approaching the Snake River Canyon. He hadn't come across another human being in all this time and was beginning to wonder whether he went the wrong way initially. (*Maybe I should have gone down river instead*), he thought, but then thought better of it. Odds were about the same in either direction. Chet also kept getting the strange feeling that he'd done something wrong. Maybe that's why he was here. (*Or maybe someone did something to me. Maybe that's why I can't remember*).

The more he thought about it the faster he walked. He could feel his blood pumping harder and harder through his veins. The more he thought about it the more paranoid he was becoming.

He was still thinking about it two days later. Then on the third day it happened. He was still making his way up the river and all at once he stopped. He could smell smoke. It took a minute for it to register what he smelled. It was wood smoke. Not like a forest fire. It suddenly dawned on him. Campers!

He dropped to the ground and slowly looked around. He was watching for any movement. After a few moments he started crawling forward trying to keep as quiet as possible. The forest was pretty dense here and provided plenty of cover. He could tell by the smell that he was getting closer to their camp. Were these the people who had hurt him?

Were these the people who had left him to die in the wilderness? Maybe they could tell him who he was. Maybe they would try to kill him!

He couldn't let that happen. He moved closer still crawling on his stomach through the low ground cover that was made up of mostly ferns and poison oak. As he came to the edge of their camp he peered through the bushes and he could see a man. The man had his back to him and was holding an axe. He was large with huge forearms. He looked like a man that was used to working with his hands. Chet looked around and saw a woman standing over an open fire. It looked like she was cooking and whatever it was it smelled wonderful. His stomach started growling so loud he was sure the couple could hear it.

He wondered if they could help him. He couldn't take that chance. What if they were bad people? (*People like that should be taught a lesson. They shouldn't be allowed to get away with what they did to him*). He noticed they had a motorhome camper. As he watched he also noticed that the camper had a large hose coming from somewhere under the unit. At the end of the hose there was a shallow trench dug in the dirt that ran away from the camper. There was some kind of blueish green sludge running from the hose through the ditch and downhill headed toward the river.

As he watched them he noticed that the man had left his jacket hung on a tree branch just a few feet from where Chet was lying. He needed that jacket. He was trying to figure out how to get it when he heard a noise behind him. He turned suddenly and saw two young children walking up a trail straight toward him. They were giggling and talking and hadn't even noticed the strange man lying next to the trail just a few feet in front of them. Chet looked around in panic. They would see him and sound the alarm.

He sprang to his feet just as they were about three steps from him. The look on their innocent faces was total shock and for just a second they froze. That was all the time Chet needed. He ran to the jacket and was reaching for it when he heard the woman and the children scream in terror and a deep voice shout, "Hold it right there."

Chet turned slowly to face the man. He was standing about ten feet away and holding the axe in both hands like a weapon. Chet slowly brought his hand around in front of him. In it was his spear. He looked the man in the eye and began to growl.

CHAPTER 6

May 8th
Washington DC

Annie sat up instantly in bed completely disoriented. (*What is that horrible noise?*) It took a moment for her to realize where she was. (*Of course, that's what it is. My wake up call from the front desk. I guess I should have skipped the Dos Equis*) She looked at the clock and saw that it was 7:01. She picked up the receiver and was rewarded with the computer generated voice dictating that it was indeed 7:01.

She sat up in bed and stretched. Then she rolled out of the bed, stood up and headed off to the shower. The room service arrived 30 minutes later as promised. It was a light breakfast consisting of fruit, orange juice, coffee and wheat toast. She was still in her robe with her hair still wet when she answered the door. After the server left she sat down for a moment and had some of the fruit, a bite of the toast, a sip of the juice and made herself a cup of coffee which she took with her back into the bathroom so she could drink it while she continued to apply her makeup and set her hair.

She decided on a pair of safari beige hiking pants with a cream colored long sleeve blouse and a pair of hiking boots. Over this she wore a brown down vest. She checked herself out in the full length mirror on the back of the bathroom door and was convinced that she looked every bit the adventuring geologist out for a rock hunt. She was sure that her traveling companions would be dressed in urban scientific geek wear including pocket protectors. Well at least one of their team would look like she knew what she was doing.

She checked the clock and saw that it was 8:20. She checked out using the television quick check out feature. Gathering her two travel bags she checked the room for anything she may have forgotten. Finding none she headed down to the lobby and walked out the front door at exactly 8:30 and was happy to see Hank standing at the curb holding open the door of the limousine.

"Good morning Hank," she said as she approached the car and got in.

"Good morning Annie," replied Hank as he gave her his best smile. "Beautiful day for a plane ride," he said as he closed her door and walked around to the driver's door. "The airport's only about 13 miles from here but in DC that means about a 50 minute drive."

"That's ok. You're right, it is a beautiful day. I think I'll just sit back and enjoy the sights."

"Is this you're first visit to the capital?" he asked.

"No I've been here a couple of times but it always looks a bit different each time I come here."

Angelina sat back and looked at the monuments and buildings as they past them.

About 45 minutes later they turned off the parkway and entered an airport through a gate that had a soldier standing guard holding an M-16 rifle and looking like he meant business. He walked up to the driver's side window and as Hank rolled the window down he stuck his head in to see who was on the inside of the car. He asked to see both of their IDs and as Hank and Annie handed them over Annie happened to look in the side rear view mirror she saw that another solder had taken up a position directly behind them although instead of having his M-16 shouldered he had his in front of him ready for action.

"A lot of security here isn't there?"

"They take their security very seriously around here." Hank replied without a hint of humor in his voice. "There's an awful lot of real important people come in and out of this place."

A moment later the soldier returned with their IDs and handed them back thanking them as he did so. He stepped back and gave them a smart salute as the gate opened and let them inside.

Hank drove around this huge base like he knew exactly where he was going and what he was doing. He passed several huge transport planes and jets as well as several rows of mean looking fighter jets that from what Annie could see were loaded for bear. She even saw one of those black sleek looking jets that she was pretty sure was called a stealth bomber. But what really impressed her was when they passed an area that had an additional security check point and was surrounded by a chain link fence topped with razor wire. Inside were about two dozen additional armed soldiers that stood in strategic locations inside the fence. Right in the middle was Air Force One. It seemed to gleam in the morning sunlight. Just seeing it sent chills up her spine.

As they continued on she could see they were heading for an area where several jets and planes were parked. It looked more like an executive parking lot than a military base. There were several limousines dropping off and picking up passengers scattered around these beautiful aircraft.

Hank pulled up next to one of the medium sized jets and came to a stop. He got out and came around to the rear door and opened it for her. As she stepped out he went to the trunk and removed her bags placing the on the tarmac next to her. When he was done he said," Well that just about does it. Hope you have a good flight." With that he turned, walked around to the driver's door, got in and drove away.

Annie stood there for a few moments looking around. (*Well now what do I do?*)

She called out," Hello?" When she got no response she tried again. "Hello?" still nothing. Was she just supposed to grab her bags and climb the steps into the aircraft? She was pretty sure that a jet like this had storage compartments for luggage.

She started slowly walking around the rear of the plane leaving her bags where they were. She had gone around the tail of the plane and was just about to the tip of the wing when a man wearing coveralls stepped in front of her. He seemed to appear out of thin air.

He was a little bit taller than her with an obviously powerful build. His hair was pitch black and he had green or maybe hazel eyes and streaks of grease on his handsome face.

As he walked up his grin widened, as though he was truly happy to see her. He asked," May I help you?"

"Yes, please. My name is Agent Angelina Cartier of the FBI and I'm looking for two men, a Mr. Malone and a Mr. Collins. They were supposed to meet me for a flight to Boise, Montana. Have you seen them?" Annie asked as she looked around for any vehicles approaching that she may have missed.

"Yep, sure have," He said as he wiped his hand off on a rag and stuck it out. "I'm Jake Collins,"

She instinctively held out her hand which he shook firmly.

"And that guy over there with his hind quarters sticking out of the cowling is Sean Malone." Jake said indicating a man on a ladder leaning with his head inside the engine compartment. "Hey Sean," he called out. "Come meet the nice lady from the FBI."

Annie looked over in time to hear the man on the ladder drop something and bang his head on the engine cover.

"Dam it." She heard as he backed out of the plane compartment.

"Jake, what is it now?" He asked irritably.

As he stepped down off the ladder he turned and Jake gestured to the person standing next to him.

Sean couldn't help himself. Immediately his face twisted into his best smile.

Annie smiled despite herself. She was looking at a man that was over six feet tall with sandy colored hair. His build was that of an athlete and she could see the strength in his arms and shoulders. But those eyes are what she noticed most. They were blue. Not just blue, but blue like the color of tempered steel. They looked like the kind of eyes that missed nothing. He held her gaze for a full ten seconds before she moved her eyes away self consciously.

"Nice to meet you ms …aah," he said as he took a rag from his pocket and began to wipe his hands on it.

"Agent Cartier," Annie retorted with a little more indignation than she meant to use. "Angelina Cartier, but please call me Annie."

"Well Agent Angelina Cartier, I'm Sean Malone and I'm sure you've already met my partner Jake Collins."

Jake grinned at her and nodded.

"We were just doing some last minute adjustments to the engine. You know what they say."

"What's that Mr. Malone?" Annie asked.

Jake spoke up." When it comes to flying there's nothing more useless than the runway behind you and the sky above you."

Sean smiled and said," I was referring to an ounce of prevention is worth a pound of cure."

"Oh yeah, that one."

Annie asked," Shouldn't the maintenance of the jet be conducted by a qualified mechanic or at leased by a licensed pilot?"

"I'm pretty sure Sean would qualify in both categories," Jake replied with a playful grin.

Annie looked at both of them for a long moment and then it began to register. "You don't mean to say that you're our pilot?"

Sean smiled and bowed as he said," Sean Malone, pilot, mechanic and cabin steward at your service."

Annie looked around to see if maybe there was a hidden camera somewhere. When none appeared she looked back at Sean and Jake and said "What have I got myself into?"

An hour later they were cruising at 420 knots and at an altitude of 27,000 ft. Annie was still adjusting to the fact that there seemed to be a lot more to her travel companions than what met the eye when Sean came strolling back from the front of the airplane. He sat down across from her in one of the leather captains chairs.

"So tell me, what's so important that it requires an undercover agent of the FBI to accompany us through the vast wilderness of the Pacific Northwest?"

Annie looked at him and asked," Who's flying the plane?"

"Jakes an amateur pilot and actually he's getting much better now that he's getting over his vertigo," Sean said with a slight grin.

She eyed him wearily as if she was trying to figure out whether he was kidding or not. After a short moment she decided that since she was to share this wilderness experience with these two guys and there was a very real possibility of danger, why not. Besides, she got the feeling that these two could definitely handle themselves in a tough situation.

"What do you know about the militias of this country?" she asked.

Sean's smile disappeared and his face took on a serious expression.

"I know that their ideals are pretty screwed up, that there are a lot of them, and that they're dangerous.

She looked into his eyes and saw something. His look went from mischievous to hard in an instant. His eyes became steely grey as he said, "Jake and I have run into several of these so called militias. They're extremists at the least. Most of them feel that you're either with them or against them, no middle. They're the worst kind of terrorists. They're prejudice bigots. The worst thing about them is the fact that their American citizens. For the most part they're not even registered and they don't vote. They think that their opinion is the only opinion. They believe that what their doing is right but they can't believe that there can be another side to their opinions."

Annie could see that this subject was very important to Sean. She decided that a serious discussion about this could wait for a better time."

"How many times have you made this journey?

"If you're asking how many times Jake and I have been to the Pacific Northwest, I'd say we've been out here maybe fifteen times, seven or eight times for business and the rest for pleasure. You could say we enjoy the mountain air. The first time I ever came to this part of the country it was with my parents when I was seven. I fell in love with the wilderness feel to the area. I think it was the feeling that I was truly in touch with nature". He sat back in his chair. "I don't think I ever got over that feeling".

Annie looked at him and was wondering if he was pulling her leg. Then she realized that he really did mean every word of it. (*Is this guy for real?*)

His gaze seemed distant for just a fraction of a moment, and then as though he realized that she was watching him he jumped back into reality. He asked," How about you? Have you ever been to the area?"

"I've been to Squaw Valley in California but other than that I've never been west of the Rockies. I've always wanted to but the opportunity never presented itself. I was born and raised in Canada and it always seemed that I was always to busy."

"I can imagine with all that Olympic stuff going on," He said with total sincerity. He had obviously been doing his homework too.

"Well, I hope this little adventure will live up to your expectations."

"I have to admit I'm just a little bit apprehensive about this assignment," She said with a look of concern on her face.

His look suddenly turned serious again and he asked, "Speaking of assignments, exactly what is it that we're supposed to be doing here?"

She thought for a moment and then began explaining. "We've been getting a lot of rather disturbing chatter over the air waves. Enough that it's got some important people worried that one of these militias may be up to something no good. They want me to try to find this group and try to infiltrate it. You know, try to find out what their planning."

He said," Boy when you decide to make things exciting you don't mess around."

"That's true, and to be perfectly honest this is my first real assignment and it's got me a little nervous. I've spent most of my carrier pushing paper and helping the Canadians watch the border trying to keep foreign terrorists out of the country."

When she was finished she waited to hear Sean's reaction to her candidness.

Sean put his head back on the headrest and thought for a minute. He looked at her beautifully sculptured face and said calmly, "You have got to be either the bravest woman I've ever met or the dumbest. Do you have any clue how dangerous it will be trying to get information about these people. Every place you turn you'll be faced with potential disaster. Most of the people in this area are militia sympathizers. Any one of them could turn you over to the very people that you're trying to investigate. Annie, these people do not play well with others. You may think their all inbred fools that couldn't tie their shoe laces without a road map but believe me when I tell you that they are anything but stupid. Most of them are well educated and their very well equipped.

Many of these organizations have complex infrastructures and will be extremely difficult to infiltrate."

Sean sat back in his chair and studied her with a concerned look.

She seemed to gain strength from his words and replied indignantly," If you feel that you and you're partner Jake up there," gesturing to the front of the airplane," aren't up to the challenge you can just drop me off and get back in the air and fly yourselves back to civilization."

With that she turned in her chair to face the window.

Sean sat there looking at her and began to smile.

(*She has guts*) He thought. (*She may not have the common sense that God gave a chipmunk but she definitely has spunk.*)

"Look Annie, Jake and I have been through a lot together and we're not about to leave you high and dry out there in the wilderness. Besides, neither one of us would be able to forgive ourselves if anything were to happen to our first FBI agent." He grinned at her with that Irish twinkle in his eye.

She looked over at him sitting there with that smile on his face and couldn't help herself. She smiled back at him and said sheepishly," I guess I'm a bit on edge."

"No worries mate," He said in his best Aussie accent. "Why don't you sit back and relax while I meander up front and see what our automatic pilot is up to," Referring to Jake.

He stood up and headed for the cockpit. A few minutes later Jake appeared and walking over to the jet's on board wet bar looked over his shoulder said," We've got a couple of hours to kill, so what's you're poison?"

Annie looked up at him and replied," It's still a bit early for me but I'd love a Diet Coke."

"Suite yourself," he said and reach down and opened an under the counter refrigerator and pulled out a Diet Coke and a Coors beer. He walked back to her, gave her the soda and asked," Mind if I sit down?"

"Of course, please do." She smiled.

After a short moment she said to him," How long have you and Sean been working together?"

"Oh hell, we've been together since Lincoln was shot."

"Pardon me?" She said looking at him with a puzzled look on her face.

"It's an old expression. Sean and I grew up together. We've known each other since our school days at Syracuse. We played football on the same team and became good friends. We've pretty much been together ever since."

She thought for a moment and then said," What can you tell me about him?"

"Sean?" he said. "He's probably the most loyal friend a guy could have. He possesses tremendous intellect and probably the best reflexes I've ever seen, even better than mine."

"I've read your files and it seems that you two of you have been on some pretty wild adventures for engineers."

"Oh that," he said smiling. "Don't hold our degrees against us. We seem to attract these types of missions. You see, besides the fact that we both have certain skills when it comes to outdoor life, Sean has something extra. He's one of those people that has that sixth sense. He's very in touch with all his senses. He can see like an eagle. His sense of hearing and smell are as acute as any dog. He can feel things like vibration long before you or I could ever feel it."

Annie was looking at him skeptically.

He went on seriously. "There's something else about him." He paused. "Sean has an ability to communicate with nature. I don't mean like Dr. Doolittle or any thing like that. It's more like he can feel it inside." He gestured with his hand to his chest. "If an animal is hurt or scared he can feel what they feel. I can't really explain it but it's pretty weird. He can stand in a forest and feel the forest. The best way I can explain it is that he's one of those people that is truly in touch with his inner self."

Jake sat back and drained his beer. Then he said, "Well, we've got about one more hour to go so if you'll excuse me I think I'll move over to the couch and take a little cat nap.

With that he moved over to the couch and true to his word within minutes was sound asleep.

Angelina sat there looking out the window and tried to digest what she had learned. She found it hard to believe and decided that it was probably just bunk.

CHAPTER 7

April 28th
Snake River, Idaho

It had been two days since his encounter with the people at the camp site and Chet was still slightly unnerved about what had happened.

Were they actually trying to harm him or were they just as scared as he was. He wasn't sure he would ever know. He was just glad that he had been able to flee with the jacket before they realized that he was just as frightened as they were.

He had continued his trek upriver checking over his shoulder constantly. He wasn't sure that they wouldn't come after him because after all, he did steal their coat.

He thought of the children. He could still hear their screams of terror in his head. That was the part that really got to him. He wondered why.

There was something in his mind that told him that children were very important to him. It was like there was something in his past. He just couldn't put his finger on it but he felt like it was important to him.

He had continued to have trouble quenching his thirst. (*Why was that?*) He wondered.

He was getting much better at catching fish with his spear. His memory hadn't improved much however, but every once in a while he got a small flashback. He remembered something about seeing a large animal right in front of them and then a sense of falling.

Wait. There was a large animal in front of "them"! He must not have been alone. But who else had been there? If only he could remember.

Chet was glad for the coat. It made the nights much more bearable, although it made him feel a little guilty. The only problem is he couldn't understand why. The man didn't look cold. Why should he have the coat when it was obvious that Chet needed it?

Oh well. That didn't matter now. The only thing that mattered was that he had to make his way up river. He didn't know why but he knew he had to.

It was about two days later that he began to notice that the taste of the water began to change. It was a very subtle change but the further up river he traveled the more noticeable it became. Probably the normal person would never notice it but when it was your life source you tended to notice the small things.

He also noticed that the wild life seemed to begin to behave differently. Wolves seemed a lot more skittish, almost paranoid. He actually saw a wolf walking down a path and a rabbit jumped out of the undergrowth in front of it and instead of attacking it immediately it was startled so badly that it ran backward for about ten feet. Of course as soon as it realized what had scared it he immediately ran after, caught and ate the rabbit. It just struck Chet as unusual behavior. Normally the wolf would have smelled the bunny from a hundred feet away.

He still felt like he had a dark cloud hanging over his head. It was like a feeling of doom. Chet had no idea why but he was certain that the answer was up river. He kept walking.

Why was he so thirsty?

While he was kneeling at the river's edge getting some water he spotted something strange. A Budweiser beer can floated by. *(Where did that come from?)* He wondered.

That could only mean one thing, "People."

CHAPTER 8

May 8th
Boise Airport, Idaho

It was just after 1:00pm local time when they landed and taxied to the area that was reserve for private aircraft.

Annie, Jake and Sean stepped down the retractable stairs onto the tarmac and just stood there for a moment to take in the view. It was truly breathtaking.

The Rocky Mountains rose far into the sky to the east of where they were standing and their snow capped peaks seemed to be watching over them as they took in their splendor.

"Magnificent isn't it," Sean said to know one in particular. "It's as if the mountains are talking to you. I never get tired of it."

Annie gazed out almost in a trance and wondered, *(Maybe this is what Jake had meant on the plane.)*

She quickly snapped out of it and automatically began looking around to make sure that no one was paying them any undo attention. When she was satisfied that there didn't seem to be anyone interested in them she began to relax a little.

Jake said," There's supposed to be an agent of Homeland Security here to meet us", as he also started to look around.

Out of no where they heard a voice behind them say," Excuse me but might you be Mr. Malone, Mr. Collins and Ms. Cartier?"

They all turned around to see a very small man. He was dressed in a brown sport coat and slacks and was wearing polished oxford shoes.

His hair was brown and receding. He wore thick glasses that gave him somewhat of an owl look.

"I'm Sean Malone, and this is Angelina Cartier and Jake Collins, and you are?"

"Oh, excuse me," he said apologetically. "My name is Cecil Barringer. I'm from Homeland Security. I was instructed to meet you and assist you in any way possible. Will you be spending the night?"

"If it's not too much trouble," Sean said. "That way we can secure a vehicle and get a fresh start first thing in the morning".

"It's no problem at all. In fact I took the liberty of booking three adjoining rooms at one of our better hotels. It's actually quite nice and it has a wonderful restaurant and bar. I've also arranged for this Ford Expedition", he said as he gestured toward the pewter colored 4 wheel drive vehicle.

"That's great Cecil", Sean replied. "And maybe you can join us for dinner".

"Very well then, shall we?" and he led them to the SUV.

Ten minutes later they pulled up in front of the Hampton Inn Hotel in downtown Boise where they were met by a pair of bellmen who promptly took their bags and directed them to the front desk.

"I'll leave you now to get settled in and I'll be back at shall we say", he checked his watch," five o'clock?"

"That'll be great", said Sean.

Jake said," I've made a list of most of the things that we're going to need to take with us". He handed Cecil the list.

"I'll make sure that everything will be ready for you by this evening". Cecil took the list, turned on his heels and headed for the door.

A little while later they were led to their rooms by a young bellman who had a wide smile for them (especially Annie) and who gave them his narrative of the city of Boise. He evidently was born here and was obviously very happy with living here. He said he had grown up hunting and fishing and explained that most of the people here were very friendly.

The young man did say that there were a couple of pretty rough bars in the downtown area that some of the local cowboys and construction workers hung out at but they were easy to spot. He said for the most part they were harmless.

Jake tipped him twenty dollars which he accepted with a huge smile. Evidently he wasn't used to getting such a generous gratuity.

After he left Annie looked around and said," I didn't realize that Homeland Security traveled in such luxury".

"We'll see if you still feel that way after a few nights out in the wilderness", Sean said with a slight smile on his face.

"Yeah", Jake said. "They like to wine and dine you right before they lead you into the lion's den".

Annie smiled. "Well, if you two will excuse me it sounds like I might as well enjoy this as long as I can". She turned and headed for the connecting door." I think I'll just freshen up and relax for a while. Besides, it'll give me a chance to check in with Washington".

"No problem," Sean said. "While your doing that I think Jake and I'll head down to the hotel bar and check out the surroundings".

"That's music to my ears", Jake replied with a grin. "When you're done you can join us".

"That sounds great. See you then". She retreated to her room and closed the door behind her.

Sean looked over at Jake who was standing there with his "cat that caught the canary" look on his face and said," Don't even go there".

"What?" Jake said with a feigned expression on his face.

A few minutes later the two of them were walking into the hotel lounge. They went straight to the bar and as they crossed the area from the door Sean took in ever person there. He did it with such subtlety that the only one that knew he was doing it was Jake. That was because he was doing the same thing.

They sat down at the bar and a pretty young bartender came over immediately and said with a friendly smile," What can I get for you two gentlemen this afternoon?" She was wearing a name plate with Jill printed on it.

As she looked at them with a bright smile of perfect teeth and a twinkle in her eye it was obvious that she liked what she saw.

Sean and Jake got those kinds of looks quite often and it always made Sean feel a little self conscious. Jake always enjoyed ever minute of it.

"Can we get a couple of Coors please", he said.

"Coming right up," she turned to the back bar and bent down to get a couple of cold beers, her tight blue jeans did not go unnoticed.

After she left the beers and headed down to the other end of the bar to help another patron Jake said quietly," Did you see him?"

"Nine o'clock, beige polo shirt with light Dockers pretending to read the newspaper", Sean said," pretty hard to miss him".

"He must be here to spot anyone unusual".

The young lady behind the bar came back over and leaned on the bar. She asked," So, what brings a couple of handsome guys like you to our little town?"

Jake said," We're scientists, here to check out soil and water conditions in the Pacific Northwest."

"Now that sounds exciting", she said sounding sarcastic.

"Yeah it can get pretty boring but where else can you get a job that makes you spend most of your time camping, fishing and just plain relaxing in the great outdoors?" He said with his best charming smile.

"I see what you mean", she said.

Jake leaned over to her and asked," Say Jill, what's with the guy over there reading the paper?"

Jill glanced over, then said quietly," Oh, I know what you mean. He comes in here every day, orders a vodka martini and sits there pretending to read the paper while he's checking out all of the customers. He never drinks his drink. It kind of freaks me out".

"How long has he been doing that?" Sean asked.

"About three weeks," she said. "Most of the staff here thinks he's one of the Keepers".

"Keepers?" Jake asked as he gave Sean a sideways glance, "What's the Keepers?"

"Their one of those militia groups that are spread out all over the northwest. You know, like one of those Branch Dividian groups except the Keepers are a lot bigger and a lot meaner. They're spread out all over the place. They hate the Government. Each segment has regular meetings out in the woods. I've never been to one but they say that they spend their time chanting and shooting. It's like the kind of stuff you see in movies. It's creepy".

"You say you've never been to one of their meetings. Do they allow women into their ranks?" Sean asked.

"Oh sure, but even the women are weird, their kind a 'butch".

At that point she glanced over toward the door and both men followed he gaze. As they did they saw Annie enter the room. She looked beautiful standing there in her camping attire and boots. She could have just stepped out of a sports magazine. As they watched she saw them and smiled. She crossed the room to join them at the bar.

Both men stood up at the same time and spread apart to allow her to sit between them.

As she sat Jill asked," What can I get you?"

"I'll have what their having".

"A beer drinker", Jake said with his best Irish accent, "tis a woman after me own heart".

Sean said quietly," We were just having a discussion about the guy sitting in the back of the room not reading his newspaper".

Annie looked at the reflection in the mirror and spotted the man.

Sean was impressed at the fact that she avoided the temptation to turn around and look. He went on saying," Jill here was telling us all about a group of people up in these parts known as the Keepers".

"Really," Annie said as she raised an eyebrow. "And what's so special about these Keepers?" She asked innocently.

"Their one of those militia groups that you read about every once in a while," Jake said.

"Really," she said again.

"Yep, and Jill here thinks that guy may be one of their spotters," Sean said.

"No kidding. And just what is it that a spotter would be trying to spot in a hotel bar?" Annie asked as she smiled at the bartender.

"Anyone from the government," Jill said seriously.

"It seems that these Keepers hate the government", Sean said as he watched Annie's eyes.

"Well, I wouldn't want to be one of those government people sneaking around here", she said.

"Me neither," said Jill. "So, are you a scientist too?"

"No, I'm more of a scientist's assistant", Annie replied glancing over at Sean who was still looking at her.

"Wow. It must be fun going out into the woods with two good looking guys like these two".

"You have no idea", she said as she looked in the mirror and saw Sean blush and Jake smile.

About an hour later and after hearing several of Jake's renditions of he and Sean's adventures Sean looked at his watch and said," Well Jill I hate to leave but we have a dinner meeting at five so I'm afraid we'll have to be getting along".

Jill, obviously disappointed leaned across the bar and said to Jake," I get off at nine".

Jake smiled broadly and winked at her. "Maybe I'll see you then", he said.

They met Cecil in the restaurant. He had arranged for a table in the rear where they could enjoy a little privacy. The restaurant was nicely decorated with white linen and crystal. It wasn't very crowded at this time of the evening.

As they sat a waiter came up to the table and handed each of them a menu. He then went through his rehearsed spiel about the specials as he poured each of them a glass of white wine.

"I hope you don't mind but I took the liberty of ordering the house chardonnay", Cecil said. "I've also asked the waiter to bring us an assortment of hors d'oeuvres".

Annie took a sip," the wine is excellent".

"It's from Napa Valley in California", he replied. Then turning to Jake he said, "I believe I've collected everything on your list. I took the liberty of having it loaded into the Expedition".

"That's great Cecil", Jake said as the waiter returned with several plates of assorted snacks.

After the waiter placed the hors d' oeuvres on the table he asked if they were ready to place their orders. Annie ordered the grilled salmon and the house salad with blue cheese dressing.

Sean ordered a New York steak and Jake ordered the full cut of prime rib and a cup of clam chowder.

They all made small talk as they waited for their dinners to arrive. When it came it was as though all three of them suddenly realized how long it had been since they last had anything to eat. The conversation stopped and they all went at their food with gusto.

When they finished their meals and their plates had been cleared Cecil, while stirring his coffee said, "Good Lord, don't they ever feed you people in Washington?"

Sean said graciously, "It's pretty rare that we're treated to a meal that tastes as good as that".

Cecil beamed at the compliment.

Annie asked him, "While we were at the bar there was an unusual gentleman sitting in a chair pretending to read a newspaper while he was watching all the people coming and going. According to the bartender she thinks he may be a member of a militia group called the Keepers. What do you know about them?"

"We've been watching them for quite a while. They seem to be ramping up for something. That fellow in the bar has been hanging around for the last couple of weeks. We've been noticing the same type of thing at other hotels, also at the airport and train station. We just don't know what their up to, but I expect the FBI will start paying them special attention".

Annie, Sean and Jake all shared a quick conspiratorial glance at each other.

Cecil went on," Well, that type of thing has nothing to do with you people. As I understand it you folks are looking for some problem with the water up here".

"Yes we are," Sean replied. "We've been told that there have been some strange occurrences up here and that it may be related to the drinking water".

"That's true but most of the reports have come in from north of here, in the area of the Snake River."

Jake said," What sort of 'occurrences' are we talking about here".

"It appears that it started with some strange animal behavior." Cecil explained. "Campers reported seeing animals being unusually aggressive. Bears, wolves and even a fox in one case, coming in close to campgrounds, that sort of thing. The National Park Service sent a couple of rangers up the Snake River to collect water samples about a month ago. They checked in at the Lewiston, Idaho station in the middle of April and sent in some of their water samples, then left to continue up the river. They haven't been heard from since".

Cecil hesitated for just a moment. "Then, a few days later a couple, camping with their two kids said that they were confronted by a strange man that snuck into their campsite and stole a coat. The husband tried to stop the thief while threatening him with an axe".

"Well that must have stopped him", said Jake with a smile.

"That's where the story gets weird", Cecil went on. "This guy is a construction worker, you know, big. He yells at this guy who's wearing torn up clothes that's trying to steal his coat and when he does the guy turns around and growls at him, like an animal. He said it really freaked him out".

"I can see how it would", Sean said.

"Any idea who the growling guy is?" asked Jake.

Cecil took a sip of his coffee. "No, but according to a description of the guy by the campers he sounded an awful lot like one of the rangers. His name is Chester Ellison. I understand that he calls himself Chet. He's a family man who has a wife and two young children. Pretty unusual behavior for a man with his background".

Sean said," That explains why we've been sent out here to check things out. The CDC reported that some of the water samples that they sent in contained raised levels of hydrochloride and benzopyrene among other things".

"What's so significant about hydro what ever you said and this benzo stuff?" Cecil asked.

Jake looked at Sean and they both said at the same time," Meth Lab".

Jake said," Well Annie, it looks like we're headed north up the Snake River".

Cecil spoke up." If you're going to go poking around in that region I would suggest that you tread with extreme caution".

"Why's that?" Annie questioned.

"Because my dear, that is one of the known stomping grounds for that militia group that we were talking about".

"You mean to tell me that the Keepers are up there too?" she asked incredulously. "Are they spread out over the entire state of Idaho?".

"The Keepers", he responded," are spread throughout most of the Pacific Northwest".

It was about 8:30 when Cecil stood and bidding them a safe journey, exited the restaurant.

They headed up to their rooms. Jake announced that he thought he'd head down to the bar for a nightcap. Obviously Jill the bartender was premier on his mind.

Angelina felt as though she needed to work off some of that delicious meal and decided to take in a night time jog. She quickly changed into her running clothes and headed out.

Sean, left with his thoughts, decided he'd take a walk down to a convenience store he had spotted on their way to the hotel. He wanted to stock up on power bars. They always seemed to come in handy.

He stepped out onto the street and headed north. The store he had seen was about two blocks up and around the corner. The street wasn't very busy and as he walked past a couple of beer joints he could hear the music from inside.

At the same time Angelina was jogging in the opposite direction. She was planning on going out about six city blocks, then circling around the hotel and coming back in from the other direction. She figured that would be about a mile.

Sean got to the convenience store and found the section that had the power bars. He grabbed about a dozen of them and went to the counter to pay for them. While he was handing the clerk the money he didn't see Annie run past the front of the store. She was on the last leg of her run and began to ramp up her speed a little. As she made the corner she came face to face with three men who had just stepped out of the bar. They blocked her path and she had to stop. They moved to surround her.

The largest of the men was built like a mountain. He had curly red hair and a bushy red beard. He was dressed like a lumber jack with a plaid flannel shirt and old blue jeans. The second guy was a little shorter and dressed similar to Curly with dirty blond hair and a smaller beard. He was built like a rock. The third man was dressed the same although he was much thinner than the other two. He had dark hair and no beard. All three of them were wearing construction boots.

The biggest one, (Curly) was in front of her. As he checked her out he said," Well lookie what we got here".

Annie immediately recognized the danger and reached back for her fanny pack which had her Glock 9 millimeter pistol in it. As she did the thin guy behind her reached out and grabbed the pack unsnapping it with amazing dexterity.

He opened it pulling out the gun and said," Well what do we got here?"

Curly leaned in close to Annie and said," Now you weren't planning to use that on us were you?"

She could smell the liquor on his breath. She looked around to see if there was anyone around that she could ask for some help. Panic was beginning to rise in her when from behind her she heard a familiar voice.

"Hey, Annie, how's everything going?"

She turned to see a smiling Sean Malone come walking up to them and slip between Rock and Skinny to place himself in the middle of everyone.

"What seems to be the problem here?" he asked.

"Mind your own business butthead", Curly said as he pushed Sean hard in the chest causing him to fall back.

Skinny and Rock both caught him, one on each arm. "You got no business here", Skinny said.

Curly raised his fist to hit Sean and as he did Sean lowered his head just enough to make sure that the blow glanced off the top of his head. Sean went down with the hit and as he hit the pavement his right foot moved to the instep of Curly's right foot while his left foot swept across his knee breaking the knee with a sickening crack.

Curly screamed in pain as the entire weight of his enormous body came down on his shattered limb.

Annie stood there shell shocked as Rock started forward with a snarl. Sean came up from the ground and caught him with the palm of his hand to his nose crushing it back into his head. He dropped to the ground out cold, blood gushing from his ruined face.

Skinny, seeing all of this reached into his pocked and pulled out a switch blade. He came at Sean with hate in his eyes. Sean side stepped his knife hand easily and grabbed him by the wrist, turning and twisting at the same time while he seemed to turn in mid air coming down on the back side of Skinny's arm with his elbow shattering his arm.

Annie, who had been watching all of this with total disbelief at what she was seeing found herself facing Skinny as he turned to run. She hauled back and swung with a perfect round house swing and knocked him out.

Sean looked at her, smiled and said," I don't know about you but I think I've had enough exercise for the evening".

"Where did that come from?" she asked gesturing to the three men lying on the ground.

"That", he said. "That's just a little something I picked up when Jake and I were in Brazil checking on the Amazon. It does come in handy some times".

CHAPTER 9

May 10th
Kalispell, Montana

John Hamilton rose from his chair at the kitchen table and slammed his hand down on the surface. "What do you mean he "thinks" they might be from the government?" he said as he eyed the man across the table from him.

"Our man Frank said that they looked like government people. He said he was sitting in the bar room at the Hampton like we told him to do when these two guys came in and sat at the bar and ordered a beer," said Jimmy Lyden feeling a little nervous.

Jimmy was one of the three lieutenants that had been called in by John. They had all been members of the Keepers since John established the order ten years ago.

John Hamilton was a 46 year old mountain of a man. He was born and raised in Crescent City, California. His father, John Sr. is where John Jr. got his size from, and most of his aggressive personality.

John's father worked for a large lumber conglomerate as a lumberjack. When John was eleven years old, disaster stuck. The lumber industry was attacked by the "tree huggers" of America. Groups like The Sierra Club began pressuring the government to restrict the lumber industry from clear cutting the American forests of the Pacific Northwest.

The government began passing laws that crippled the industry. Jobs began to dry up and John's father was laid off. It didn't take long for the money to dry up and John's father started to drink heavily. Soon he was coming home every night drunk and violent. After a while he started hitting John's mother. This went on for a couple of months and finally his mother couldn't take it any longer and she left. She never came back and John never saw her again. His father continued with the drinking and with no one else around, he turned his violence on his son. John Jr. found himself dreading his father's arrival each evening.

One night when he was twelve his father came home even more drunk than he usually was. He walked through the door and began beating John Jr. with the buckle end of his belt, hitting him over and over and screaming at the top of his lungs. It was all John could do just to protect his face from the lashing. As his father began to tire he began to stumble. He swung the belt just as John ducked and his father lost his balance. When he fell the back of his head hit the front edge of the stone hearth knocking him out.

When John reached down and touched his neck he could feel his old man's pulse. He grabbed his dad by the hair and began slamming his head against the stone over and over.

He stood up and looked down at his father's dead body. Then, out of anger, he kicked him in the ribs as hard as he could.

He turned and walked out the door. He never looked back.

He spent the next few years picking up odd jobs working around some of the lumber mills that were still operating. Because of his size he was rarely challenged and when he was he showed a tremendous ability to fight. He had gotten his viciousness from his father and his hate from the government. They had taken away everything that he ever cared about.

He had seen how the government had restricted the fishermen from not over fishing the salmon from the Klamath river yet that same government allowed the "American Indian" to spread their nets across the mouth of that same river where it met the ocean and take as many of the fish as they wanted. It was a double standard in John's eyes.

By the time he turned eighteen he had devoted his life to doing everything he could to get back at the establishment that took his young life away.

John Hamilton would get even.

He spent the next couple of years organizing a group of people, mostly men, who felt the same way he did regarding the government. They all felt that government was trying to establish a dictatorship and in order to do that the first thing they would have to do was disarm the people of this great nation.

Not on their watch.

They began amassing a huge amount of money and weapons. People started joining their organization from all over the Pacific Northwest. Soon their numbers were in the thousands.

John decided that if this country was going to survive, they were going to have to keep their God given rights. That's how he came up with the name," The Keepers".

Jimmy went on." Frank said that a woman joined them at the bar and they all started talking quietly to this bartender girl and every once in a while they would sneak a look at him

"That's it? That's all he's got on these three?" John asked as he looked around the table.

"Frank said that after a while they went into dinner and met with a," Jimmy checked his notes. "Cecil Barringer. He's a local representative from Homeland Security".

John's eyebrows lifted as though someone had said the magic words. *(The Government)*, he thought.

"Was there anything else this Frank had to share?"

Jimmy said, "He said that afterward, when they had left the dinner table he asked the waiter, who is one of us, what they talked about. The waiter said that they were very cautious of what they said when he was at their table but he was able to pick up small parts of their conversation. He said they were talking like they were scientists and it had something to do with the water. He took it that they were headed up north of Boise into the mountains".

John thought for a moment. "Al," he looked over at the man to Jimmy's right. "You better send out an alert to our camps up in those regions to be on the lookout for these three scientists. The last thing we need is some Ivy League types to stumble across something when we're this close to accomplishing our mission".

"You got it John", Al responded.

"I think I'll take a run down there and have a little look around just to make sure we've got our backside covered. Hank can come with me", John said as he looked over at the third man at the table.

Hank had known John longer than anyone else. He was a big man, almost as big as John, with long dirty blond hair and a bushy beard. He was also almost as mean as John and had gotten a reputation as the enforcer for the organization. He was ruthless.

"Great, we'll leave in the morning at nine".

CHAPTER 10

May 10th
Snake River, Idaho

It seemed like he'd been walking for years. Chet kept thinking that just around the next bend he'd find all the answers.

He was still getting small flashbacks, mostly while he slept. There weren't any huge breakthroughs but they were definitely coming more often.

He remembered driving fast down a dirt road. He remembered seeing three deer, no, bigger than deer. They were elk, three of them, just standing there, right in the middle of the road. He remembered thinking, *(OH MY GOD, WE'RE GOING TO HIT THEM)*. Then there was a loud noise. Someone was yelling. He could hear himself yelling," We're not going to make it"!

Now they were tumbling over and over. The other guy fell out of the car. No, he was thrown from the car. The noise is ear splitting. Then there's nothing, no noise, he's falling. Down he goes, and he's going to die.

Chet wakes up suddenly, breathing hard, sweating. He looks around and sees that he's still in the forest. The night chill is still in the air and he shivers, not from the cold but from the dream. He's had this same dream for the last couple of nights. He's pretty sure that it's not a dream. He's sure that it's something from his past, but what?

He can't figure it out but he knows the real meaning of it is up ahead, up the river.

He stands and walks down to the river. He NEEDS a drink of water badly. He's got his spear with him. He never goes anywhere without it.

When he's finished drinking he stands and steps out on to a rock, waiting for breakfast. Here it comes. He stands poised and just as the fish swims by the rock he strikes.

Breakfast is served. He's figured out that cooked fish tastes a lot better than raw fish.

He's gotten pretty good at making a fire and soon he's sitting on a rock enjoying his meal.

When he's done he puts the fire out and begins his daily routine of walking up the river.

The day is mild. Not a cloud in the sky. As Chet walks along he thinks that under different circumstances this might be a real nice way to spend a day, but not today.

Chet's on a mission. He's got to find out who the owner of that beer can is. The trouble is, there's no way of knowing how far that can had floated down the river. The only thing that Chet is certain of is that can came from up river.

As he rounds a bend in the river he comes across a Bull Moose drinking from the riverbank. When the moose spots Chet he jumps back as if startled. Normally a wild moose would have heard him coming from a thousand yards away.

As the moose regains his composure it's as if he realizes that he's a fourteen hundred pound beast and here is this measly little one hundred and ninety pound creature with a stick trying to scare him. So he does what any proud monster would do, he charges.

It didn't take Chet long to figure out that this was not going to be pretty. He dropped his spear and ran for the tree line. As he ran he could hear the animal coming fast. He was looking for the biggest tree he could find. He knew that if the tree wasn't big enough in diameter, the moose would knock it down like it was a twig.

He was now about thirty five feet into the tree line and he spotted it. The tree had about an eighteen inch trunk. Chet would have liked it to be bigger but beggars can't be chooser, especially when you've got the beast from hell crashing through the forest behind you and all he wants to do is crush you into the dirt.

Chet hit the tree at a full out sprint and began scurrying up the branches as fast as he could, and it was none to fast because as his foot cleared the ten foot mark the moose crashed through the underbrush and hit the tree at full force.

The entire tree shook. The impact almost caused Chet to lose his grip on the branches he was holding on to. He was sure that the tree was going to fall over, but it held.

The enraged beast glared up at him with a menacing look and blared. He took about five steps back and rammed the tree again, but it still held stubbornly.

This went on for another half an hour before the moose decided that this was getting boring. He finally gave up. Chet, his heart still pounding, stayed in the tree for another hour, just in case the monster was just being sneaky.

He couldn't figure out why the moose had attacked like that. Normally they were pretty mild mannered. Their temperament was a little like a horse. Sure they had been known to attack if someone got too close and spooked them, and they could always be dangerous during mating season.

But this attack was actually vicious. It was as if the animal was deranged. It was pretty strange behavior for a moose.

What was even stranger was how would he know how a moose should behave? It must have something to do with his past.

When he was pretty sure that the moose had left, he quietly climbed down from the tree and continued walking up the river in search of the litterbug.

It was just about dusk and Chet was starting to look for a good spot to bed down for the night. He was still walking along the tree line so he went down to the water for a drink.

He noticed that the fowl taste in the water was getting a lot stronger. It was kind of bitter and now he could smell it. It smelled a little like rotten eggs.

As he stood up at the river bank he caught a smell in the air. *(Is that smoke?)* He wondered.

Yes, but not wood smoke like a campfire. The smell was almost acidic. What ever it was, it wasn't a smell that belonged in a forest.

He hurried back up to the tree line and started making his way forward slowly. As he followed the river it made a slow bend to the right. It was wide at this spot and it gently flowed past him.

Then he saw it. It was a cabin. No, it wasn't a cabin. It was more like a mobile home, out here in the middle of nowhere. It had a small shed off to one side of it. Like a wood shed. There was also a white pickup truck. It was a white Ford F-250 about ten years old Chet guessed although it was hard to tell because it looked like it had never been washed and the right front bumper was primer grey.

Chet didn't know why but his gut told him that something wasn't right. He dropped to the ground. He was slowly crawling forward toward the home when the door slammed open and two burly men came out. They looked like fat hippies One was a little taller than the other.

Chet was still about one hundred and fifty yards or so from them but he could still make out some of their conversation. They each had a beer in their hand. It was Budweiser, just like the one in the river.

The bigger one said," Well, that batch should bring in about twenty five thousand".

"Yeah it should," the shorter one said as he took a pull from his beer. "This sure is a tough way to make a livin."

"Sure is," the other one said and they both laughed out loud.

"Say, where's Charlie gone off to?"

"I don't know," the taller one said as he took a drink from his beer. "He's probably off taking a leak in the river".

Chet was trying to inch his way a little closer so he could hear more of what they were saying. He was trying to be as quiet as possible. He didn't know what these guys were doing out here but he was pretty sure that they were dangerous.

As he slid forward on his stomach he heard a branch crack behind him. He started to turn toward the noise when something hit the back of his head. The last thing he saw was a large dark shadow. Then his world turned black.

CHAPTER 11

May 9th
Lewiston, Idaho

The three of them had been driving for about three and a half hours. Each one of them had taken a turn.

Jake and Sean had even reluctantly let Angelina have a turn. Neither of them were used to leaving the driving to anyone else but they both had to admit that she was pretty proficient behind the wheel.

Sean figured that the best place to start was where the two rangers were last seen. He wanted to try to find out what had happened to them.

They had all discussed this on the way.

"I think if we can find them they can help us find out what's going on up here", Sean explained.

"Sean those two guys went missing over two weeks ago", Jake said. "Do you think their even still alive?"

Annie spoke up. "I pulled both of their files last night in the room. They've both been with the rangers a long time. Their record shows them to be very experienced and skilled when it comes to anything to do with surviving in the forest. These guys are pros".

Sean asked," How'd you get their records that fast?"

"Membership has it's privileges", she said with note of pride in her voice. "Chester Ellison, who goes by Chet, joined the National Park Service in 1983. He obviously has the most experience. His partner, Andy Franklin is younger. He's been with the Service for a little over ten years but both of them have been doing field work for pretty much their entire carriers. These two were definitely not beginners".

"I wonder what happened to them", Sean thought aloud.

Annie said," They have a satellite phone with them and both of them have cell phones but nobody has been able to get a hold of them. They even called Chet's wife to see if she's heard from her husband. She hasn't and she's worried sick. Their both armed with hand guns as well as high powered rifles".

"According to the Park Service they even tried to find them by trying to lock on to their phones using satellite tracking but so far they haven't had any luck".

Sean said," Well, let's start with the last people who saw them".

"That would be Ranger Jack Mathews at the Lewiston Station", Annie said. "He's the one who runs the show up here".

They pulled into the Lewiston Ranger Station at about eleven and asked for Ranger Mathews. They were told that he was down at the diner having an early lunch. They were given directions and they headed that direction.

When they walked into the diner everyone in the place seemed to stop what they were doing and looked up at the three strangers. They obviously were not used to seeing a lot of new faces around here.

The three of them had no trouble spotting the big ranger. He was wearing his uniform and sitting with another uniformed gentleman in a booth about five tables from the front of the restaurant. They seemed to be having a conversation with a pretty young waitress.

The waitress immediately got Jake's attention who looked at her and gave her his perfect teeth smile. This did not go unnoticed by Annie who looked at Sean who just shrugged his shoulders as if to say "what are you gonna to do?"

As they walked up the waitress moved away and Jake's eyes followed her. Annie elbowed him in the ribs and he looked at her sheepishly and grinned.

They turned their attention back to the ranger and Sean saw that the man with him had a sheriff's badge on. Both of the men where wearing guns.

"Excuse me but are you Ranger Jack Mathews?" Sean asked.

"That's right, and may I asked who you three are?"

Sean made the introductions. "My name is Sean Malone. These two are Angelina Cartier and Jake Collins. We're with Homeland Security".

Sean didn't want to give away the fact that Annie was actually with the FBI. He knew that up in these parts anyone could be and probably were members of the Keepers.

Both men stood up and the ranger extended his hand as he said, "I'm Jack and this other guy here is Sheriff Wallace Murphy".

The Sheriff stuck out his hand and shook each of theirs. The two men were both several inches taller than Sean.

Jack said. "Why don't we move over to a table and we can all have a cup of coffee".

The waitress immediately came over with three mugs and a coffee pot and began pouring.

"Thanks Jenny", he said as she placed napkins and spoons in front each person.

"My pleasure Jack", she said with a smile. "The more the merrier", and she went over to help the other diners.

The Sheriff said, "So what brings you folks way up here".

"We've been sent up here to check the water system. There have been some reports of some strange happenings in this area and the government wants us to check the water to see if there's anything wrong".

The sheriff seemed to take note at the mention of the government as he said, "I don't think we have any problem with our water. You want to be extremely careful what you say. We wouldn't want any unnecessary gossip to spread about water contamination. If the people of this community got wind of three people from Homeland Security nosing around about our water system it could start a panic".

Sean looked into the man's eyes and he thought he saw something disturbing about the way he was looking at them. It made the hair on the back of his neck stand up and Sean had learned along time ago to trust his instincts.

Jake spoke up. "Sheriff we're not here to cause a ruckus. Sean here is a Chemical Engineer and I'm a Hydro Engineer. We're scientists who just happen to work for the government. Annie here is with the CDC. The last think we want to do is get people all riled up".

The Sheriff eyed him suspiciously. "And what about you", he said as he gestured to Annie. If word gets out that you're from the Centers for Disease Control that'll start a panic for sure.

"Sherriff, as far as anyone is concerned just tell them that I'm their assistant," she replied.

"You mean to tell me that you need someone from the CDC to go out and get water samples?" he said incredulously.

Jake said, "Have you got any idea of the amount of paperwork the government requires to take even one sample, let alone test an entire water system".

"Why without Angelina here we'd be buried up to our elbows in forms and documents", Sean said sincerely. "We'd be lost without her".

The Sheriff looked at her a little too long as Annie held his gaze.

(Secretary) She thought, *(You backwoods hick)*

The Sheriff stood and said, "Well at least try to be discreet". As he turned to head for the door he said to everyone, "If you'll excuse me I've got to make my rounds. Jack, I'll see you later", and he walked out the front door, without paying for his coffee or leaving a tip. This did not go unnoticed by Annie. *(It figures)*

Sean looked over to Ranger Jack and said, "He's a little gritty isn't he.

Jack said, "Who, Wally? He's ok. He just lets the badge go to his head. Now, what can I do for you three".

Jenny came back over and asked if they would like to order anything. They all ordered some lunch and she left to place the order.

Sean asked the ranger, "Jack, what can you tell us about the two rangers that disappeared?"

The ranger looked at all three of them and it was as if a light bulb went on. "You're here because they disappeared". He paused then went on, "There really isn't that much to tell. They were real nice boys. They were assigned to take water samples up the Snake River to Yellowstone. They stopped here to send some of the samples they had collected to the CDC and we had breakfast in this diner".

"Did they seem alright? I mean did they act as if anything was wrong?"

"No. The only thing they did report was that they had an unusual encounter with a grizzly".

"What kind of encounter?" Jake asked.

"They said that the bear acted pretty aggressive. They said it was unusual behavior even for a grizzly which by nature is a bit on the aggressive side. We went out the next day to check it out but we couldn't find the animal".

"Was there anything else?" Sean asked

"No", he went on. "I did tell them about some campers that had been attacked". He went on to tell them the story.

When he was through Annie asked, "What did the autopsy show?"

"Not a lot. It appeared to be an animal attack but they haven't got the DNA back so everything is pending on that. In the mean time we've been trying to increase our patrols but we're short handed and there's a lot of country to check out".

Their lunch came and everyone ate quietly, as if they were all thinking. When they were done Sean said, "The samples they sent back had some traces of hydrochloride and benzopyrene. There was also a little chlorine, like bleach."Jack, have you heard any reports up here having to do with Methamphetamine?"

"You mean as in Meth Labs? Yeah we've had some reports to be on the lookout for that type of activity but we haven't seen anything up to this point". The ranger thought for a second. Then he said, "Do you people think there may be a connection between drugs and our missing rangers?"

Jake said, "We can't rule it out. With the existence of those chemicals in the water and the disappearance of those guys, it sure sounds like quite a coincident".

Sean said, "It could also explain some of the strange animal behavior too".

"So where do we go from here?" asked Annie.

"Looks like we're going camping," replied Jake.

CHAPTER 12

May 11th
Lewiston, Idaho

John Hamilton and Hank Mire rolled into Lewiston about noon. As they drove through town they spotted the sheriff sitting in his car on a side street just off Main Street.

They pulled up and the sheriff rolled his window down.

"Afternoon Wally," John said with a smile.

"We've got a problem. Actually we have three problems", said the sheriff as he scowled back at them.

"What's got you so spooked?" asked John.

"We've got three government people just showed up in town two days ago asking questions about our water. Two of them are scientists and they brought their secretary".

"They brought a secretary to check out a river?" said John with a note of disbelief.

"She's quite a looker if you know what I mean," the sheriff said with a slight smile."She's actually an agent with the CDC. She suggested that we refer to her as their secretary so as not to worry the folks around here. It seems they were sent by Homeland Security to check out the water system. It has something to do with contamination".

"What sort of contamination are we talking about here?"

"The kind of contamination that comes from three idiots operating a meth lab alongside a river," replied the sheriff. "Evidently they've been getting reports about animals acting strange so they sent two rangers up the river to take water samples".

"Yeah, so what's the big deal?" John asked as he pulled out a cigarette and lit it. "Those guys have got the lab set up all the way on the other side of Hells Canyon part way up the mountain".

"Well it seems these two rangers came through here a couple of weeks ago and dropped off some of the samples. Then they headed on up the river and haven't been heard from since", said Wally.

"So what, you think our guys had anything to do with them disappearing?" This came from Hank who was sitting in the driver's seat.

"I doubt it. Those three couldn't tie their shoes without a road map", replied Wally as he watched a young lady cross the street pushing a baby carriage.

John asked, "So where are these three government people now?"

"They left the same day heading up river".

"Well, just call Charlie up there and tell him to pack up everything important and then torch the lab", said John. The fire will take care of any evidence including DNA".

"That's one of our problems John. There's no way to reach them up there on that mountain. Cell phones don't get a signal".

John thought for a moment. "Which way did these scientists and their girl friend go?"

"They took the fire trail that follows the river. I'm guessing that their either going to try and find those rangers or their going to try to find out what happened to them or both".

"How long do you figure it'll take them to make it to the lab?"

"It'll take at leased two or three days," answered the sheriff.

"Well that settles it then. Hank and I will take Hwy 95 and head straight for the lab. We'll spend the night here and leave early in the morning. We should be able to get there by noon. By the time those scientists get there all they'll find is ash".

"What about the water?" Hank asked. "When they test the water, their bound find chemicals in it".

"Big deal," John said. "They'll probably figure it was just kids trying to make some money. After the fire there won't be one once of evidence that'll point them at us".

"There's one other thing you should know about," said the sheriff quietly.

"What's that?" John asked as he flicked his cigarette butt out the window.

"There's this young kid in town," the sheriff went on. "His name is Billy Joe Sanders. He does some odd jobs for us like run supplies up to the lab".

"Yeah, so what's the problem," John asked impatiently.

"Well lately he's been doin a lot of drinkin down at Danny's Bar. He gets drunk at night and try's to show off how important he is to the organization. You know, for the ladies".

"What's this Billy Joe been saying?" questioned John.

"He's been telling them and anyone else that's within ear shot how important he is to the Keepers. How he's the one that makes sure that everything at the lab goes smoothly". Wally went on, "He keeps talking about how he's the one setting up the Big Plan to get back at the government".

John's ears turned crimson as he said, "what time does this kid usually show up at the bar?"

Billy Joe Sanders was a big kid. He was a little over six feet tall and weighed out at about two hundred twenty pounds. He was twenty three years old and his pock marked face and the scabs on his arms gave away the fact that he was a regular user of the meth they were making. He had grown up in the Lewiston area where his father had been a potato farmer. He had never been known as a very smart kid. He never graduated from high school and didn't have many friends.

The only job he'd ever had was when he joined the Keepers and began to be a "runner" for them.

He spent most of his days sleeping in his bed at his parents' farm. He was a creature of the night.

Tonight was the night he thought he would be able to impress those two young girls that had been coming into Danny's.

Maybe he'd even get lucky. To prepare himself he took a extra hit of meth, just to keep himself alert.

He got down to the bar at about 7: pm and by 8:30, had himself pretty well primed and ready for when the girls showed up.

There were quite a few people in the bar and the noise level was high as people strained to talk over the music playing from the electronic juke box in the corner.

At 8:35 John Hamilton and Hank Mire walked in the front door. Everyone in the bar seemed to turn in unison and then everyone stopped talking.

They were quite the imposing sight. Everyone knew who they were and what they represented. They were revered by many and feared by some.

They stood there for a moment as John scanned the room looking for the person they had come to see. He saw him standing toward the back of the bar and as John started to walk that direction Billy Joe looked up from his beer and saw the two of them approaching.

He did a double take as he recognized who they were. Then he stood up straight, smiled meekly and said, "Mr. Hamilton, sir", and stuck out his hand.

John held his gaze and looked down at the man's hand not taking it and said, "We need to talk".

The man sitting at the end of the bar was Dan Childers. He knew John Hamilton well and was also a member of the Keepers. It was no coincidence that he was also the owner of this establishment. He gestured toward the back and then got up and started heading that direction. He led them down a narrow hall to a storage room that doubled as an office. John and Billy Joe followed with Hank taking up the rear.

Childers opened the door with a key, turned on the light and then stepped aside to allow the three of them to step past him. He then followed them in, closed the door and locked it with a deadbolt.

The room had an old four legged wood table with four wooden chairs around it and a single light bulb hanging from a chain over it. John walked around the table and sat in the chair that was opposite the door as he gestured for Billy Joe to sit in the chair across from him. Dan sat in the chair to John's right.

Hank stayed standing with his back to the door.

Billy Joe looked around the room nervously twitching his eyes. He was all too aware of Hank right behind him.

John just stared at him for a moment.

"Wha…what can I do for you Mr. Hamilton", Billy stammered.

John leaned forward and rested both of his muscular forearms on the table as he said, "Billy Joe, I've been hearing some things about you that are very disturbing".

"Wha…wha…what kind of things", he said nervously, his eyes still darting around.

"It seems you've been doing some bragging about the organization and what you do for us", John said as he stared into Billy's eyes.

"It's just bar talk Mr. Hamilton. I don't mean anything by it. It's just conversation".

"You mean to impress the ladies", John said this as a statement.

"Yes sir," Billy Joe said as he began to relax.

"I understand that you also said something about the "Big Plan" to these ladies", John gestured with his fingers making mock quotes.

"It was just bar talk, honest", Billy pleaded crossing his heart and holding up two fingers like it was a Boy Scout pledge.

"Billy, just how much do you know about the Big Plan and who else have you told about it?"

"Nothing, really", Billy said. "It's mostly just rumors mainly, something about hitting the government where it'll really hurt them. I haven't told anyone else".

"You sure Billy," I wouldn't want to find out later that you lied to me", John said this in a fatherly tone.

"I swear to God, Mr. Hamilton. I haven't said a word to anyone else".

John smiled at Billy and made a move like he was dusting a piece of lint off the calf of his pants.

The move was so fast that if you didn't know it was coming you would have missed it. John's hand came swinging back up in a blur. In it he held a hunting knife with a ten inch blade. The knife came down with tremendous force and pinned Billy Joe's hand to the table.

It took Billy a moment to realize what had happened. He looked down at his ruined hand, and then his nerves sent a signal to his brain.

The music in the bar was turned up high enough that no one heard the blood curdling scream that came from the back room.

Hank, who was still standing behind Billy stepped forward and grabbed the back of Billy's head by the hair. Then his right hand had

Billy by the chin and with a powerfully violent move wrenched Billy's head around and with an audible crack his scream was silenced. He released Billy's head and it lolled to the side as the life left Billy Joe Sanders.

John sat back in his chair for a moment and then turned to Dan Childers who had sat through this without any expression and ask, "Dan, who were the girls that this idiot was shooting his mouth off to?"

Dan said, "Just a couple of young gals who appeared to be out to enjoy a fun night on the town. I don't think they were paying any attention to him".

"You ever see them before?"

"Nope, that was the first time I've ever seen them. They looked like they just turned twenty one".

John sat there thinking for a moment, and then dismissed it. He looked to Hank and said, "We better get some sleep. We've got a busy day tomorrow".

Julie Delaney and Anna Barnes had been sitting at the bar since nine fifteen and so far hadn't seen that spaced out Billy Joe guy.

"I don't think he's going to show up tonight", Anna said quietly as she took a sip of her beer.

"Let's give him another fifteen minutes", replied Julie.

"Ok, but not a minute longer. This place gives me the creeps".

Julie and Anna were both a little over thirty years old, although you'd never know it. They both looked like college grad students. That's why they had been picked for this assignment.

Both were undercover agents for the Drug Enforcement Agency (DEA) and had been sent here to try to find out about a potential methamphetamine lab somewhere in this area.

So far, courtesy of Billy Joe, they had found out that there was a lab but they hadn't found out where it was yet.

The DEA had been informed about the chemicals found in the water by the CDC. They needed to find out where it was before they could move in and make a bust.

"He either had to make a run to the lab or something happened to him," said Anna.

"Yeah, or we've been made and their just setting us up," said Julie as she scanned the bar for any unusual activity.

"Let's get out of here and call in our report," whispered Anna as she started to stand.

She turned and stepped right into a hugh man. It was like hitting a brick wall. Hank Mire stood there blocking her path.

Anna was a seasoned professional and immediately went into her teenage tipsy routine.

"Oops, excuse me," she slurred as she turned back to Julie. "I'll be right back. I've got to go potty", and then she giggled.

Julie, never missing a beat said, "Me too. I'll go with you", as she stepped down off the stool nearly knocking it over. Then she giggled too.

Hank looking disgusted stepped aside to let the two young drunks get by. *(If their daddy only knew what they were up to)* he thought, then turned and headed out the door.

CHAPTER 13

May 10th, 2012
Hells Canyon, Idaho

They'd spent the night along the Snake River. Annie had even tried her luck fishing. She caught her first fish and decided she was pretty good at it but she drew the line at cleaning it. *(Yuck)*

Sean and Jake had set up three one man tents and started a small camp fire. It was early in the season and the fire risk was almost non-existent. Still they were very careful to pick out a nice open area, ringing the fire with large river rocks.

After dinner was over and the dishes were cleaned and put away the three of them sat around the small fire and relaxed.

Annie sat back looking up at the night sky that twinkled with so many stars that it looked like a scene from Disneyland.

"I could get used to this," she said to no one.

"I never get tired of it," said Sean following her gaze.

"It's ok, but give me Las Vegas," said Jake with a twinkle in his eye.

"Ignore him," replied Sean to Annie. "He wouldn't give this up for all the show girls in Nevada".

Annie smiled at them both. She couldn't get over how well these two worked together. Although you didn't have to be around them very long to realize that they had a special friendship, the kind of friendship that two brothers might have.

She said, "I placed a call to headquarters while you two were setting up the camp".

"And what did HQ have to say?" asked Jake.

"They said that they got a memo from the DEA regarding your mysterious chemicals. It seems that while we were in Lewiston the DEA had a couple of agents there checking things out. They were there posing as college grads on vacation and they ran into some guy that liked to drink and brag about how important he was to some organization. How he spent his time running supplies to a meth lab".

"You're kidding," said Sean.

"And get this, they found out that the organization running the meth lab was some militia group".

"Don't tell me, let me guess. The Keepers", said Jake as he looked over to Sean.

"Well now we know where at least some of their funding comes from", said Sean.

They all sat there quietly thinking as they stared into the fire. Then Annie spoke up.

"One other thing the DEA told us was that this kid said something about the "Big Plan.". He bragged about how this Big Plan was going to show the government that they meant business".

"I wonder what kind of thing they could do that would shake up the government", Sean said to no one in particular.

Annie said, "I don't know but I think it just became even more important that we find these rangers and this meth lab".

Sean stood and lifted his head up to see the stars. He took a deep breath and thought *(this is not good)*.

"Well I think it's time for me to get my beauty sleep", said Jake as he yawned and stretched.

"Me too," agreed Annie, "sounds like it's gonna be a long day tomorrow." She stood up and started to turn to head for her tent.

"Annie FREEZE," Sean whispered in a harsh tone.

She had been a cop long enough to understand that phrase. She froze in mid stride and looked over at Sean. His eyes had become intense and he seemed to be looking past her. She glanced over at Jake and he too was looking at something beyond where she was frozen. She slowly turned her head to see what it was that drew their attention. When she did she saw a massive tree about ten feet behind her. *(But wait)*, she thought. *(There wasn't a tree behind her when she sat down)*.

As that thought began to register in her mind the tree moved. Her eyes slowly moved up and she found herself looking into the eyes of the biggest bear she had ever seen. He was standing on his hind legs and stood well over twelve feet tall. As she stood there frozen the bear looked down at her. He curled his lips back and roared. The sound was defining.

Annie was sure she was going to pee her pants as she stood there fighting the urge to scream Then she heard Sean's voice. "Stay where you are and don't move," he said as he slowly stepped around her to stand between her and this ferocious beast.

The bear was about fifteen feet away. Annie looked over at Jake who was slowly making his way to the back of the truck.

(He's going for a gun) she thought as she held her breath.

Without looking Sean said quietly, "You too Jake, just stand still." He continued looking at the bear and said in almost a gentle tone, "He's not going to hurt us. Something has him scared."

Annie thought, *(he's scared, right!)*

Sean stood there staring at the animal for what seemed to be an eternity. The bear finally got back down on all fours and began pawing at the ground like a bull in a bull fight. While he was doing this his eyes stayed locked on Sean's.

To Annie the bear looked menacing. As she watched Sean continued to stare into the bear's eyes she heard him say softly, "It's ok big guy. Nobody's going to hurt you."

The bear roared again but this time it seamed more like a reply than a threat. Annie couldn't believe what she was witnessing. The bear seamed to be communicating with Sean and vise versa.

After a few more minutes of this the bear seemed satisfied that he'd spoken his peace and turning slowly he began heading back into the forest.

Sean stood there for several minutes watching the bear's retreat. Then he slowly turned around to see Annie standing there with her mouth open gawking at him. He looked over at Jake who was standing about six feet from the back of the truck. Jake looked over at Annie and he grinned as he said to her, "see what I mean."

She came out of her trance and asked incredulously, "How did you do that?"

Sean shrugged his shoulders and said simply, "I didn't do anything. That bear was just afraid that we were here to invade his territory. Once I reassured him that we meant him no harm he was satisfied. I think we better get some sleep. Like Jake says, he needs all the beauty sleep he can get."

Sean and Jake headed off to their tents leaving her standing there speechless, looking back and forth between the direction the bear went and Sean. *(Unbelievable).*

CHAPTER 14

May 11th
Snake River, Idaho

Chet woke up with the headache from hell. When he opened his eyes his vision was so blurry that all he could make out was a light bulb that seemed to be magically floating over his head. He tried to move his head but when he did it sent a stabbing pain to his neck. He tried to reach up with his right hand to rub his neck but something was wrong there too. He couldn't move his hand. He tried his left hand and found it wouldn't move either.

(Oh my God) he thought, *(Am I paralyzed)*. He felt himself starting to panic. He began to stand up and he found he couldn't move his legs. *(I AM PARALYZED)*.

His heart was pounding so hard that he was sure it was going to explode from his chest like something from an Alien movie.

His vision began to clear and he looked down at his hands. They were being held in place with duct tape, so were his legs. He was tied to a wooden chair with duct tape.

He was caught between elation that he wasn't paralyzed and the fear that he was tied down to a wooden chair.

Where was he? He remembered lying on his stomach watching a couple of fat hippies drinking beer outside a mobile home, then hearing a noise, then pain, then nothing.

Wait a minute. The noise he'd heard must have been the third man, the one they called Charlie. He'd snuck up on him from behind and he must have hit him in the back of the head with a club or a heavy branch.

But where was he now? That's right, he realized. He must be in the little building that was next to the mobile home, the wood shed.

It was all starting to make sense. But why was he duct taped to this chair. All of a sudden he realized that his cloths were gone. All he had on was his underwear. Why'd they take all of his clothes? Then it dawned on him. They must be doing something illegal and they think that I'm here to arrest them. So why didn't they just run away?

(Their going to torture me to find out who else is coming to bust them)

Now Chet was beginning to panic again. He struggled against his restraints but it was no good. No wonder people always say *if you want to do a job right, use duct tape.*

He sat there trying to figure out a way to cut himself loose. Maybe he could use his teeth. No, they had wrapped the duct tape around his chest to hold him in an upright position. As he sat there he heard voices. They were coming.

He tried to hear what they were saying and as they got closer he could make out most of what they were talking about.

"He's been out since last night. I think you hit him too hard. He's probably got one of them concussions," said the first voice, obviously one of the two fat hippies. He must be talking to the one they had called Charlie.

"He's lucky I didn't just beat him to death," said Charlie as they stopped just outside the shed.

"Well, what are we going to do with him now?" asked a third voice.

"We're going to try to wake him up and find out what he was doing out there sneaking around. When Hamilton finds out about this he's going to want some answers."

Chet heard a heavy chain rattle and then the door flew open letting blinding daylight flood into the shed. The three of them entered then they closed the door behind them.

"Look here, he's awake," said the shortest one as he stood there smiling.

"Well, let's get started then." This came from the one they called Charlie. He was larger than the other two and clean shaven. He was dressed in jeans and wore a flannel shirt and construction boots. He also wore a no nonsense frown on his face. This guy meant business.

Chet realized that these men weren't wearing masks, and neither was he. That could only mean one thing. *(They don't care if I see their faces)*, he thought as they came closer. *(I'm not getting out of here alive).* He started to panic again and began to struggle against his restraints.

"What are you people doing here and why am I tied to this chair? What's going on?"

Charlie walked up to him and backhanded him across the face. The move was shocking and painful. "We'll ask the questions punk," he yelled into Chet's ear. "Who the hell are you?"

"I….I don't know," he said truthfully.

"Bullshit," he bellowed as he slapped Chet's face hard with the front of his hand this time. It felt like being hit with a club. "Who are you?"

"I'm telling you the truth; I don't know who I am."

"Bullshit," he yelled again. This time he punched him right in the solar plexus.

Chet leaned forward as far as his restraints would allow and retched.

Charlie continued, "I'll ask you again. Who the hell are you?"

Chet was trying to think of something to tell this maniac before he pounded his guts into pulp. He looked up with tears in his eyes and pleaded, "I'm telling you the truth. I don't know who I am."

Charlie hauled back, this time with his fist and hit him just above his left eye. The blow was so powerful that it snapped Chet's head back and he passed out.

"Now look what you've done," said the larger of the two hippies who had been standing back smiling. "You've gone and killed the son of a bitch."

The smaller of the two hippies walked up to Chet and felt his neck. "Gnaw, he's still alive. He's just passed out."

"When he comes to, we'll start phase two of the interrogation."

When Chet regained consciousness he was even more disoriented than he had been before. He was still strapped to the chair and the light bulb was still suspended overhead. The only difference was that now his left eye was swollen shut. He could taste blood and it felt like he had a loose tooth.

He heard the chain on the door rattle and then the door swung open. This time the two fat hippies came in first. One of them was carrying a shallow metal wash pan while the other followed with a five gallon bucket of water. Both were grinning like two kids at a pony ride.

(What, were they going to give him a bath?) Chet thought. The thought scared him almost as much as that Charlie guy.

As if on queue Chet looked back to the door and there he was. He had a car battery with him and a pair of jumper cables.

Chet was starting to get a very bad feeling about this.

As if Charlie could read his mind he smiled and entered the shed setting the battery down about five feet away.

"We're going to teach you how to speak when you're spoken to," he said unrolling the cables.

"I already told you," Chet pleaded. "I don't know who I am."

"We'll see if we can jog you're memory," Charlie said as motioned to the other two.

They moved toward Chet with the biggest one stepping behind him. Big fat hippie grabbed the back of the chair and leaned him back while little fat hippie slid the wash pan under the front of the chair. Then they set the chair back upright placing both of Chet's bare feet into the tub.

Little fat hippie then took the bucket of water and poured it into the pan filling it with about five inches of water.

Charlie said, "Now comes the fun part," as he attached one end of the black jumper cable to the metal edge of the pan. The other end he attached to the battery. Then he attached the red cable to the battery. "Sure hope this works," he said with a slight chuckle.

He moved toward Chet with the end of the red cable.

No one was within five miles of that mobile home. If there had been anyone they would have wondered what kind of animal could scream like that.

CHAPTER 15

May 11th
Hells Canyon, Idaho

Jake was driving while Angelina rode shotgun and Sean sat in the back. The rest of the night had been uneventful and they'd all woken up at about six thirty. By seven thirty they were packed up and back on the road. At least that's what they had started calling this dirt fire trail.

It was about ten o'clock and the sky was clear and blue. They were following the river and Sean was taking in the sights.

The trail was rough and dusty as Annie looked over and said, "Jake, are you actually aiming to hit every pot hole in Idaho?"

"What, like you could do any better?"

"My grandmother could do better," she quipped.

"I'll have you know that my specialty is driving cross country. I've even won races. I've got trophies to prove it."

"I wonder how many bribes that took," she said sarcastically.

"Ok kids, do I have to separate you two," said Sean from the back seat. He was starring out the passenger side window looking at the river below. As they rounded a bend in the road he yelled "Jake stop!"

Jake, not knowing what was wrong slammed on the brakes coming to a skidding stop and throwing Annie forward against her seat belt.

"Sean," she said irritably. "What the hell…"

Before she could complete her sentence Sean threw open the back door of the Expedition and jumped out as the vehicle came to a stop.

Jake was out his door almost as fast. Annie was still fumbling with her seat belt as Jake asked, "What is it Sean?"

"Look at this," he said as he led Jake to the edge of the dirt road. He crouched down at the edge of the drop off and starred at the surroundings.

Then Jake saw it. It looked like tire tracks But they weren't heading on down the road. They were heading off the edge. They were both looking over the edge down toward the river below as Annie came over and stood next to them.

"What is it," she asked following their gaze.

"It looks like somebody missed the turn and went over the edge," Jake replied. "Look," he said pointing down the hill side.

"You can see where the vehicle rolled all the way down hill until it got to the shear cliff down there," Sean said pointing out the broken trees that made a path.

"Could that have been the rangers?" Annie asked.

"Smart money would bet on it," said Sean as he checked out the surroundings. He continued, "It looks like they came around this bend," he paused as he moved backed to the road, "and by the look of these tracks there was some kind of deer or elk in the road."

He walked toward the edge and said, "They swerved to miss it and went over the edge."

"Oh my God," said Annie. "You mean they went down there?" pointing down into the ravine.

"That's what it looks like," said Sean.

"Well, what are we going to do now. We've got to find out what happened to them."

Jake said, "Well, that means someone is going to have to climb down into that canyon and find out what happened to those people.

Jake looked at Sean. "Heads or tails?"

"Heads," Sean said.

Jake produced a coin and flipped it, catching it one handed and slapping it down on the back of his other hand. "HEADS", he announced as he frowned and headed to the back of the Expedition. He pulled out ropes and climbing gear then walked to the edge and began his decent.

The first one hundred feet down was steep but not so steep that he needed any of the gear. He went down about three quarters of the way then stopped.

"You got anything," Sean yelled down.

He walked off to the left and disappeared into the trees. A moment later Sean and Annie heard, "I got a body."

Sean stood up from his crouch, "Annie, you turn the truck around to face the river." As she went around to the driver's side Sean went to the rear and pulled out his own set of climbing gear and a collapsible stretcher. He went back over to the edge and called down to Jake, "I'm coming down."

He waited as she maneuvered the large vehicle into the right position. When she had it sideways on the road facing the edge he grabbed the wench cable and hit the release button. With the cable in one hand and his climbing gear in the other he went over the edge heading for Jake.

When he got down to him, Jake was checking the man's pockets. At leased he thought it was a man. It was obvious that the body had been here for a while. It was going to take DNA testing to determine who this was.

Jake pulled out a wallet, opened it and read, "Andrew Franklin, National Park Service, Well, it looks like we found our missing rangers."

"One of our missing rangers," Sean corrected. Then he looked around and said, "Looks like this guy was thrown from the car as it rolled down the hill. The car itself kept going, right over the edge."

"Holy crap," Jake said as he thought of the other ranger still in the vehicle going over the edge.

"Let's get this guy out of here. Then we'll see if we can find the other guy."

They placed the body on the stretcher and attached the wench cable to it and yelled up to Annie to begin bringing him up. As the body of the ranger began to ascend gently up the slope Sean and Jake turned and headed down hill to the drop off.

They each belayed their ropes off to a tree about ten feet from the edge and threw the rest of the rope out over the canyon.

Jake looked over the edge. "Looks like about seventy five feet or so."

"Going down is always the easy part," Sean said as a matter of fact.

They each attached their ropes through a brake bar and using carabineers attached them to their descendeurs. Then they went to the edge, turned, and yanked once hard on their equipment just to make sure everything was secured. When they were confident it was they started to back up and went backward over the edge.

They repelled down the face of the shear rock wall stopping about every twenty five feet to install pitons into the rock face to help with their return trip back up.

Ten minutes later they were standing on the bank of the fast moving river. They both stood there for a couple of minutes catching their breath and taking in their surroundings.

There was no sign of the vehicle. "If I had to make an educated guess, judging by the depth of the river at this section, I'd say that their SUV is out there on the bottom."

Jake said pointing to the middle of the river.

"Jake. Check out at the bank on the other side of the river. It looks like some of their stuff floated up on the shore."

They both started to make their way up river climbing over large rocks as they did so. About a thousand yards up they came to a section where the water had to go between five large boulders. The large rocks were about five or six feet apart and it was fairly easy for them to jump from one rock to the other to get to the other side of the river.

When they got there they began to hunt for clues as to the whereabouts of the second ranger. They found wood shavings, like someone had been sitting there witling while they watched the river flow by.

Then they found the dead carcass of a fish. It looked like an animal had eaten it raw.

They walked up to the tree line and saw where someone or something had made a bed in the pine undergrowth. They also found droplets of dried blood.

They saw footprints leading up river from there.

"How long ago did Annie say these two rangers disappeared?"

"About two weeks ago," answered Sean.

You don't suppose that the ranger actually survived the crash and is wandering up the Snake River do you?"

"I don't know but it could answer the question about that family that was camping. You know, the ones that had their coat stolen." said Sean.

"Yeah," said Jake, "but that doesn't explain about the thief growling at them."

"I hear you there," replied Sean.

"But why growl at them? Wouldn't ithave been easier to just asked for their help getting back?" Jake wondered aloud as the two of them stood there starring down at the river.

"I don't know but if I'm not mistaken that sounds like a helicopter. Annie must have called the Park Service as soon as the body was pulled up. We better get back and let them know what we found down here."

It took them about half an hour to climb back up the canyon wall and crawl back up the hill to where Annie was waiting. When they were almost to the top they heard the whop, whop, whop of the helicopter as it moved off back toward Lewiston.

They told her what they had found at the bottom of the ravine.

She told them that the helicopter crew had lowered a ranger and a litter by cable because they were unable to land in such rough terrain.

She also told Sean that they were expecting a call from him when he returned from the river.

Sean made the call immediately and told them what he and Jake had found.

When he was finished with his report he disconnected the call and returned the phone to the Expedition.

"What's our next move?" Annie asked.

"I think we should keep heading up river and try to find this ranger before he finds this Meth lab. Those kind of people don't usually enjoy hikers dropping in on them.

Annie went to the back tailgate of the SUV and said, "While you two were down there romping around the countryside I was able to download pictures of the two rangers. This is the one we're looking for, the one they call Chet."

As she said this she turned her laptop screen so they could see the screen.

Seeing his face seemed to put a sense of urgency into all three of them and they began to pack up everything as quickly as possible.

Before seeing what he looked like they were just looking for a ranger. Now they were looking for a fellow human being. A man who was in trouble and needed their help, because that man didn't know it but he was headed into a den of rattle snakes.

CHAPTER 16

May 12th
Meth Lab
Snake River, Idaho

John and Hank parked on the gravel directly in front of the mobile home. They'd left at 6:00am and it had taken them five and a half hours to get there. They got out of the car and both of them stretched as they took in their surroundings. It was obvious that they had beaten the government team here.

Charlie and the two hippies were sitting on the front porch of the double wide mobile home drinking beer with their feet up on the rail.

As the two men climbed the stairs to the porch Charlie said, "Hey John, Hank. What brings you two all the way up here?"

John said, "Three people from the government are headed up the river in this direction. I've decided it's time to shut this operation down."

"That might not be necessary," Charlie said.

"What do you mean?"

"Let me show you." Charlie stood up and walked down the stairs toward the wood shed with John and Hank following.

"You ain't gonna believe this," Charlie said as he pulled a key from his pocket, unlocked the padlock and removed the chain on the door. When he opened it and went in John and Hank followed. The first thing they noticed was the smell. It smelled like a sewer.

As their eyes adjusted to the darkness they saw a naked man duct taped to a chair. He had obviously been beaten and his upper torso looked like he had been burned. His head lolled to one side.

"Is he dead?" John asked moving a little closer.

"Nah, he's just passed out,"

John leaned over to get a closer look at his face. "Who is he?"

"I don't know. He wouldn't tell us. I figure he's gotta be a government agent," Charlie said. "No normal human being could have taken what we did to him without breaking."

Hank looked at John and said quietly, "I wonder if this guy could be one of those rangers that disappeared?"

"Could be," said John. "Charlie, when did this guy show up?"

"I caught him spying on our operation the day before yesterday."

"Well he's not one of the three government people I was talking about, that's for sure. They wouldn't have been able to make it here that fast."

"What are we gonna do with him?" Charlie asked.

"Go get those other two idiots on the porch and have them haul him over to the lab."

John told Charlie. "We'll put him in there and then we'll torch the entire operation. When those government people get here they'll find his remains and figure that the druggie went and blew himself up. It'll take'm weeks to find out that it was really one of their lost rangers. By then we will have been able to complete the Big Plan at the Columbia."

They moved out the door to get away from the stench and headed over to the porch where they sat down and had a beer.

After they left, Chet opened his one good eye and looked around frantically trying to find some way to get out of that dam chair. *(Their going to burn me in that mobile home.)*

He started struggling against his restraints but it was no use. They wouldn't budge. Then he heard more noise as someone approached the shed.

Again he dropped his head to his chest and pretended to be past out. He was afraid that if they found him awake they'd bring that battery back in. He wondered who those two new guys were. The one they called John was the one who gave the order to burn him.

The three of them sat on the porch drinking their beers as they watched the two hippies carry Chet into the mobile home. He was still duct taped to the chair and passed out.

John said, "We should try to make it look like the place blew up on its own."

"That's easy enough to do," said Charlie as he took another beer out of the cooler. "All we have to do is turn all the burners up in the lab. Eventually they'll overheat. Then glass starts to break and all those nasty chemicals start to mix together. When that happens, they create a really explosive gas. The gas hits the burners and there you have it."

"How long do you figure it would take?"

"Probably thirty to forty minutes."

John looked over to Hank who gave a slight nod of his head in approval. "OK then, let's do it."

They all finished their beers as the two hippies came back out. Charlie informed them of their plan and the two of them started grinning like school boys. All three of them went back inside to gather what few belongings they had. They brought them out and started throwing them in the back of their pickup truck.

John and Hank went over to their car as they watched Charlie head back inside to set up the explosion. The two hippies grabbed the lawn chairs and the cooler from the porch and headed back to the truck.

When Charlie stepped back into the lab he saw Chet fighting to get free from the chair. Chet started yelling, "You can't do this. I didn't do anything. Please, let me go," he pleaded.

Charlie went to the counter and grabbed a roll of duct tape. He ripped off a piece and walked over to Chet. Before Chet could say another word he slapped the tape over Chet's mouth. "That otta shut you up," he said as he laughed and started turning on all of the burners.

Chet watched in terror as Charlie finished up, turned, smiled at him again and walked out the door.

"That'll do it," he said to John and Hank as he headed for the pickup. "You've got just over a half an hour to clear out."

"That should give us plenty of time. The smoke's bound to draw in the fire fighters and we don't want to be anywhere near here when they start bringing in their firefighting equipment. They'll have the roads all blocked up," John said to Hank and without another word they both climbed in the car and drove off heading north.

CHAPTER 17

May 12th
Meth Lab
Snake River, Idaho

It was five minutes after John and Hank had pulled out when Sean, Jake and Annie rounded a bend in the dirt fire trail and came upon a mobile home.

They had been taking water samples as they went. They found that the chemicals were getting much stronger the further up river they traveled.

Couple that with the missing ranger and they knew that it was becoming more and more urgent that they get to this Meth lab as soon as possible.

They were driving fast and as they came around the bend Sean slammed on the brakes coming to a complete stop. All three of them sat there looking at the home.

"Do you think that could be our Meth lab?" Annie asked no one unparticular.

"That's a strong possibility," Sean answered as he took in the entire area. "Alright, here's the plan. Jake, you take one of the rifles and head out on foot into the trees on the left. You should be able to get close enough to cover us as we approach the home. Annie and I will pull up and get out by the front porch. We'll act like a couple of campers asking for directions. If we see anything that confirms that it's the lab, we back off and call in the troops, Any questions?"

"Yeah, how come I'm the one that has to hoof it through the forest while you two get to drive up?"

"Because you're a better shot than me," Sean said as he grinned at Jake and as he turned away he winked at Annie.

Jake considered that for a couple of seconds, then nodded his head and said, "That's a fact."

Jake got out of the SUV and went to the rear. He opened the hatch and got out a rifle and a box of cartridges and then he walked back around to the driver's side window.

"OK, give me about five minutes to get into position and for God's sake, be careful."

"You too, buddy. And don't forget our motto."

"All for one…"

"Not that one,' said Sean.

"What motto is that?" asked Annie from the passenger seat.

"Don't get shot."

"Jake, if you do have to use that," she said pointing to the gun, "try not to kill them. We need witnesses to interrogate."

"You got it." He turned and headed off into the trees.

As Annie watched him disappear into the forest she said, "I hope he knows what he's doing with that rifle."

"Who, Jake?" Sean said with a slight grin. "You don't have to worry about him. He could take a tick off a dog's back at one hundred yards. He always hits what he's aiming at. Speaking of guns, would you reach in the glove compartment and hand me that gun."

Annie opened the glove compartment and pulled out a 357 Smith and Wesson revolver and handed it to Sean. He checked it quickly to make sure it was loaded, and then he slid it into his belt at the small of his back.

"I would have taken you for a semi automatic kind of guy," she said as she checked her own gun, slid it into her front waist band and zipped up the parka she was wearing to hide it.

"The revolver is more reliable, never jambs."

"I like having more bullets," she said smugly.

"I try to hit what I'm aiming at," he said with a grin.

Sean started the engine and put it in drive. "Let's go see what their cooking up in there," and he began to move forward toward the mobile home.

As they pulled up about fifty feet in front of the structure Annie said quietly, "It doesn't look like anyone's home."

"Looks can be deceiving. If their in there I can guarantee they don't want company."

They both got out of the car and cautiously approached the front porch.

Sean looked at Annie and nodded. She called out, "HELLO," and she started up the steps to the front door. "HELLOOO," she called out again while Sean kept an eye on the windows.

She knocked on the door and said loudly, "Is anybody home? I'm afraid we're lost and we were hoping you could give us some directions."

She turned to Sean and shrugged her shoulders, "I guess nobody's home."

Inside the mobile home Chet was trying with all his strength to break the bonds that held him to the chair. He was almost out of energy when he heard a noise. Had they come back, he wondered? Maybe they had changed their minds. No, he thought. They had left for good. They had left him to die.

The reality of his death was starting to sink in. Then he heard knocking at the front door. Someone was out there. He had to warn them. Somehow he had to let them know that this hell hole was about to blow up.

How? How could he get their attention?

He began rocking the chair he was strapped to back and forth. If he could make enough noise they'd hear him. He was trying to yell at the top of his lungs but with the tape over his mouth it was just a muffled mewing.

He continued to rock, harder and harder. He could feel the chair rise to the top of its apex. He was going to fall over. He braced himself for the impact and as he started to go over his shoulder hit a table and a couple of beakers that were on it slid off the edge and hit the floor at the same time he did. When they did they exploded throwing splinters of glass in all directions.

Outside the front door Annie and Sean were trying to figure out what they should do next. She knew that they didn't have a warrant. That would take some time. She reached for the door knob and tried to turn it. It was locked. She looked at Sean and asked, "What do you think we should do?"

As she stood there waiting for Sean to say something he stopped moving. He tilted his head to one side. It was an awkward move. A little like a dog might do when it hears a high pitch whistle.

He said, "Did you hear that? It's like a whine. It sounds human."

At that moment they both heard the crash of glass breaking.

Sean never missed a beat. He took a half step back and slammed his right foot onto the door next to the door handle. The door jam splintered as the door swung inward. Sean reached behind his back and in one fluid motion he had the gun in front of him. At the same time Annie had her gun out holding it two handed in the firing position.

Sean went in first sweeping the gun across the right side of the room while Annie was right behind him sweeping left.

"Clear left," she called out after checking for bad guys.

"Clear right," Sean said after doing the same.

They were standing in what would have been the living room of the mobile home, although by the look of this room it looked more like it was were they kept their livestock. It smelled like a cesspool. It looked like a fast food dump. There were pizza boxes and hamburger wrappers spewed everywhere and Annie was sure she saw one fast food bag from a popular burger place that had "Over one million sold" written on it. How old would that have to be, she wondered?

Sean heard that noise again. It was coming from the next room. They cautiously entered the room and immediately knew they had found the Meth lab.

There were tables lining the outside walls where Brunson burners were cooking beakers full of different colored liquids. There were tables spread all around the room that were covered with baggies and food saver machines. Some of them had empty beakers and vials on them.

As Sean scanned the room he saw movement in the corner of his eye. He looked over and saw a table turned over and he could see what looked like the top of a head that was partially blocked by the table. The head moved. Sean pointed and he and Annie moved to each end of the overturned table cautiously looking around the edges.

It was a man. He was duct taped to an overturned chair. Sean could see the man's eyes. They looked at him wildly, almost frantically. He was almost completely naked and he had duct tape over his mouth. That was the mewing sound he had heard. The man was trying to scream through the tape.

As Annie moved closer she was able to get a closer look at the man's face. "Sean, check out his face. This guy's been beaten."

Sean reached down and grabbed the corner of the duct tape covering his mouth and quickly pulled it completely off.

Ignoring the pain of having the tape pulled off, the man immediately started yelling, "You've got to get out of here. This place is about to blow!"

"What are you talking about?" Annie asked as she moved in closer to him.

"They've rigged this place. All those chemicals are over heating. I heard them say that when those beakers break the chemicals will mix and then explode."

Annie looked at him thinking he just might be delusional but Sean looked up and scanned the room. He immediately understood and reached into his pocket pulling out a pocket knife and began quickly cutting the duct tape holding the man to the chair. "Annie, we've got to get him loose and get out of here."

As she began ripping at the tape beakers began exploding from the heat.

"There isn't enough time. You two get out of here," cried the man.

"Not without you buddy," Sean said as he cut through the last wrap of the tape.

He and Annie yanked the rest of the tape off and Sean quickly pulled the man to his feet. He wobbled and started to go down.

"I can't, my legs won't function."

Sean grabbed him by the shoulders and heaved him up and over his shoulder as more and more of the beakers were breaking. They could see the noxious vapors beginning to rise from the tables.

"Let's get the hell out of here," Sean yelled as Annie turned and started to run for the front door with Sean, carrying the man over his shoulder, was right on her heels.

They cleared the door and took the stairs down two at a time. Annie, who was running faster, began to increase the distance from Sean who was still carrying the man.

She saw movement to her right and realized it was Jake running toward them. "Jake get back!" she yelled. "It's going to blow."

Jake seeing the panicked look on her face started back stepping away.

Annie had made it about one hundred feet away but Sean, moving much slower with the extra weight, had only made it about fifty feet when his world exploded.

CHAPTER 18

May 14th
Calgary
Alberta, Canada

John and Hank had driven for a day and a half to reach Calgary. They both had their passports with them so crossing the border had been no problem. This meeting was set up to begin finalizing the plan.

They met at a log cabin just south of Calgary. It was set back from the road and looked like it had been there for a hundred years, which it had.

When they walked in it was easy to see that the place had been upgraded within the last few years. It was two stories and had four bedrooms. Each of the bedrooms had a private bath. It had obviously been designed to be a hunting lodge although it had all of the comforts of a modern hotel including a stainless steel kitchen and a large flat screen TV in the grand room. The room was decorated with the heads of many of the animals that could be found in this part of the country.

There was every thing from a silver fox to a mountain goat with its large curled horns and a bull elk with a huge rack of antlers. There were ducks, pheasant and even quail among the trophies.

There was even a huge stuffed polar bear in one corner of the room. It was standing up on his back legs showing its massive teeth as though it was attacking. It had a brass plate on the base that it was standing on that said "SHOT BY WAYNE JOHNSON OCTOBER 1994".

If anyone looked closely at the bear's front torso they could count at leased twelve patches from bullet holes. No single person went out hunting for polar bears. There was always a guide and as many as twelve guests of the person who was picking up the tab for the hunting party. That person always got the first shot, after which the rest of the group would open fire on the large animal.

Jimmy Lyden was already there along with Al Jessop. Wayne Johnson from Calgary, who was the host, was also present and the last man was Red Dunn from Spokane.

Johnson said to Dunn, "I assume you received the last of the shipments."

"Yep I sure did. We've got it all locked up in a warehouse not far from the train station."

Johnson looked over and said, "John, are you sure a thousand pounds will be enough?"

"Al's the demolitions expert," John said. "What do you think Al?"

"I think with a thousand pounds of C4 I can make one hell of a hole in the ground." Al looked like a kid that just got a new toy.

"Well we're not trying to make a hole in the ground, we're going to bring the United States government to its knees. When this facility is brought to the ground it'll rock the whole country," John said. They could hear the excitement in his voice. "Those political assholes in Washington DC are going start paying attention then."

"Well it took twenty families six months to get that much across the border. I just hope it was worth it," said Johnson.

"It's our job to make sure that their effort was worth it" This came from Hank who sat there starring at the other men.

John said, "Jimmy, were you able to pick out some competent men to serve as support?"

"We've got ten of our best. Actually it's eight men and two women. They've been training at our compound in Butte for the last six months. Their ready," He said this with a note of pride in his voice.

"What about weapons?" John asked looking at them all.

Red Dunn spoke up, "everyone will be armed with MP5 machine guns and two of the men will carry grenade launchers. Oh, and I almost forgot. They'll also have a couple of SAMs, just in case."

"What's a SAM?" Lyden asked.

"It's a shoulder fired surface to air missile", Red said with a grin.

John thought for a moment and then said, "Well it sounds like the plan is coming together nicely."

"John," Wayne Johnson said, "don't you think it's time you told us just exactly what we're going to blow up?"

"Not quite yet. If anyone gets picked up I don't want to take the chance that the government could find out what we're about to do. We've all worked way to hard to screw it up now. In four days I want the entire team assembled at the warehouse in Spokane. That's when we'll go over the final plan and everyone will find out what our objective is. Until then everyone is on a need to know basis. Is that understood?" John looked around the room and everyone nodded in agreement.

"Good, then I'll see you all in four days," he said in dismissal.

When they had all left John heard footsteps coming down the stairs and asked, "What do you think?"

The man walked over to the wet bar and put some ice in a glass. "I think everyone will do exactly like you told them John," he said as he poured Black Velvet Canadian Whiskey into the glass and walked over to a chair by the fireplace. "Every one of those guys hates the government bureaucracy just as much as we do," the man said with a rare show of emotion. "Their dedicated to the cause and they believe in what we're doing."

"Yeah," John said. "But are they dedicated enough to give their lives for the cause if necessary?"

"I don't think there's a single one of them that doesn't believe in what we're doing here. They all believe that the United States government has gotten to the point that it's lost touch with the people."

"That's right. This will be the shock that'll make them sit up and pay attention to the voice of the people. They'll find out that we're not about to stand back and let them destroy our country."

CHAPTER 19

May 12th
Meth Lab
Snake River, Idaho

Flaming debris was falling all around them as Sean tried to shield the man from the explosion. He felt someone pounding on his back. He turned over and held up his arm to protect himself from the blows. It was Jake.

"What the hell are you doing," Sean yelled.

Jake's lips were moving but Sean couldn't hear a thing. The noise from the blast had deafened him.

As his hearing started to come back he could hear Jake saying, "I said you were starting to look like a Baked Alaska. Your coat was on fire.

Sean got to his knees and tore the coat off as Annie came running back. She dropped to her knees in front of him and took his face in her hands.

"Sean, are you alright?" she asked with a genuine note of concern in her voice.

Sean grabbed her by the shoulders, looked into her eyes and with a boyish grin said, "Annie I'm fine, my hearing's even coming back."

She couldn't help herself. She rapped her arms around him and kissed him. He gently pulled away and held her by the shoulders as he examined her face. What he had first thought were bruises turned out to be just dirt.

He asked, "What about you? Are you ok?"

"I'm fine," she said sheepishly as she realized what she had done. "I just got the wind knocked out of me."

Jake, who was standing over them, cleared his throat and said,"I'm fine in case anyone's wondering."

They all looked back at the burning structure. "Jeez Sean, how come you blew that place up?"

Sean and Annie looked at each other and just rolled their eyes.

There was a groaning noise and they turned back to see the man had woken up and was rubbing his head.

Annie leaned over and brushed the hair from his forehead.

"Chet? she asked looking down at his battered face. "Chester Ellison?"

"Where am I," he groaned.

Chet was sitting on the tailgate of the SUV. Jake had given him a pair of blue jeans and a T shirt with a big yellow smiling face on it and a caption that read "Have a nice day". Sean gave him a pair of his tennis shoes that seemed to fit pretty well. Annie was administering first aid to him.

"What day is it?" he asked her, "and who are you guys?"

Annie looked at Sean, then looked back at Chet and said, "It's Saturday, May 12th."

Sean spoke up, "I'm Sean Malone and that ugly guy over there is Jake Collins. We're from Homeland Security, and this lovely lady is Agent Angelina Cartier of the FBI."

"Chet, what can you remember?" Sean asked him. "Do you know what you were doing out here?"

Chet took a deep breath and said, "We were told to get water samples along the Snake River. I remember driving along the river on a dirt fire trail. Andy was driving. He was going real fast, too fast and as we came around a bend in the road there were three elk just standing there in the middle of the road. He swerved to miss them and we went over the edge."

His eyes were starring out at the surrounding forest as he continued to remember.

"We were rolling down the mountain toward the ravine. Andy's door flew open and he…. Wait," he said suddenly sitting up straight. "Where's Andy?" he asked with a tone of desperation in his voice.

Sean put a hand on his shoulder and gently said, "Chet, Andy didn't make it. We found his body in the forest just above the ravine. It looked like he died on impact."

Chet slumped back down. A tear rolled down his cheek.

"I told him he should slow down." He looked up, "I told him," and his voice drifted off.

Annie who was sitting next to him gently put an arm around him as he sobbed.

Sean and Jake looked at each other and said nothing.

"After a few moments Sean said, "Go on Chet, what happened then?"

"The SUV rolled over and over. Then it went off the edge, airborne, still rolling, into the ravine. It hit the water upside down and began to sink. Water was rushing in from everywhere. It was so cold. Somehow I managed to get out of the vehicle. I remember being in the rapids, then my head hit a rock. The next time I woke up I was lying on the shore."

"I didn't know how I got there. I couldn't remember anything, not even my name."

He went on for the next half hour telling them how he fished for food and how something made him continued up river. How the water tasted funny and how he couldn't get enough of it.

"I think that when you hit your head on that rock it caused a form of temporary amnesia," Sean explained. "Maybe the explosion reversed that effect."

Sean went on to tell him how the chemicals in the water could have affected his mind. How it could tend to cause delusions and paranoia.

Chet continued, telling them about the wolf and how he came upon the family camping.

"I guess I'll have to buy that guy a new coat," he said almost jokingly.

He went on to tell about running into the moose and how it had reacted. How he came upon this place and how they had captured him and tortured him.

"It was the guy they called Charlie, he's the one that did most of the torturing. He kept asking me who I was and what was I doing up here? I kept telling him that I couldn't remember who I was but he wouldn't believe me. The other two guys, the ones that looked like two fat hippies, just stood there laughing. Those fat bastards, if I ever see them again," he let the sentence die off.

"This afternoon these other two big guys showed up. I was pretending to be past out because I didn't want them to use that car battery on me again, God that hurt."

"One of them they called Hank. He looked real mean. He didn't say much. The other one they called John. He was big and mean looking too and I got the feeling that he was the boss. I heard him say something about the Big Plan. He was concerned about how three government people weren't going to interfere with his Big Plan at the Columbia."

Sean, Jake and Annie all looked at each other.

Chet went on,"Then this John guy told them to put me in the house and burn me."

He told them to set it up to make it look like a druggie blew himself up.

"Then they all left and that's when you people showed up. I don't know how I'm ever going to repay you."

"We're just glad that you're all right," said Annie.

Chet asked, "Do you guys have a phone that works out here. I have to call my wife to let her know that I'm all right. By now she's probably worried sick."

Jake gave him the satellite phone and the three of them stepped away to give him some privacy.

"He'll have one hell of a story to tell his grandchildren," Jake said.

"I'm just glad he'll be around to tell it," Sean said with a smile.

CHAPTER 20

May 13th
Snake River, Idaho

They decided that the best course of action would be to bed down for the night and get a fresh start in the morning.

They gave Chet Sean's tent and sleeping bag and Sean slept in the back of the SUV with the blankets they had brought.

The next morning Sean was the first one up so he started a fire and made a pot of coffee. While it was brewing he sat down on a log and took in his surroundings. He loved this time of the day.

The sun was just starting to break through the trees and there was still a bit of night chill in the air. The forest was quiet except for the occasional squawk from a nearby blue jay out looking for an early morning breakfast. He could smell the forest around him. He could feel it.

He heard rustling behind him and turned to find Annie standing in front of her tent stretching and yawning. She even looked beautiful first thing in the morning he thought.

She came over and sat down on the log next to him.

"Good morning," he said quietly.

"Good morning, is it coffee yet?"

"Just about," he replied scooting over a little to make room. "Did you sleep well?"

"I slept like a rock, although I did wake up a few times thinking about these Keepers and this guy John. Do you think he's really crazy enough to do any serious damage?"

Sean thought for a moment. "Annie, I think that anyone or any group that's deranged and mean enough to tie a person to a chair, torture that person and then try to burn him alive is nuttier than a fruit cake and capable of just about anything."

They sat there for a long moment just looking and listening to the forest around them.

Finally Sean said, "Isn't it magnificent?"

"What's that Sean?"

"All of this. I mean Nature itself. It's so complex yet so simple."

"I'm not quite sure I understand," Annie said as she looked over at him.

"What I mean is something like this," he said as he reached down and picked up a pine cone and held it up. "When you look at this, what do you see?"

"I see a pine cone," she said trying hard not to sound too sarcastic.

"I know that but it's not just a pine cone. It's a seed. It's nature's way of reproducing.

It's survival, in the purest form. When a female grizzly bear, possibly the most ferocious animal in the western hemisphere, or at least one of the most ferocious has a cub she nurtures it and protects it with a tenderness that only nature can produce."

"I think I understand what you mean," she said. "Sean, how were you able to communicate with that grizzly bear?"

"I don't really know. It's been that way for as long as I can remember. When I was young my parents brought me out here on a trip to Yellowstone."

He went on to tell her about his early morning fishing excursion.

"I remember watching that girl washing her hair with shampoo right there in the lake. I remember how shocked and appalled I was, how angry it made me. Then when that buffalo came crashing out of the forest I realized that it wasn't my anger that I was feeling. It was the buffalo's anger. I should have been terrified but instead I was feeling what he felt. It was pretty weird."

I told my parents about it and my mom, she was a botanist, explained that some people have the ability to feel things that others can't. She told me that some plants can feel danger, a little like when a tree senses a logger coming toward it with an axe in his hand. Some people have a sort of sixth sense. I guess I'm one of those people."

"All I know is that was the most amazing things I've ever witnessed," she said.

Jake stuck his head out of his tent and whispered, "Is breakfast ready yet, I'm hungry enough to eat a bear."

"It will be as soon as you get your butt out of bed and cook it," Sean replied in good humor.

As Jake walked up and sat down on a log opposite them he asked, "So what's up?"

"I was just asking Sean what he thought of these Keepers."

"If you ask me, I think that whole brunch are about one beer shy of a six pack," Jake said.

Sean stood up, picked up a towel and grabbed the coffee pot from the grill that was placed over the fire. He handed a cup to Annie and another one to Jake filling both of them with the steaming dark liquid. Then he poured himself a cup and sat back down.

She held the cup to her nose taking in the rich aroma as she cooed, "Hmm, that smells wonderful."

"It'd smell a lot better if it was wrapped around some ham and eggs," Jake quipped.

Chet came out of his tent rubbing his eyes. He sat down on the log Jake was sitting on and Jake handed him a coffee cup.

"Thanks," he said as he yawned.

They watched as he took the towel and grabbed the pot to pour himself a cup. As he poured his hand was shacking and they all made a point of looking away to avoid embarrassing him.

They sat there quietly sipping their coffee for a couple of minutes.

Finally Sean said, "I get the feeling that we're running out of time. I think we better head back to Lewiston. We can drop Chet off at the local hospital so he can be checked out by a doctor. Then we can ask around and see if we can get any clues as to where this John and his buddy Hank were headed to."

Chet looked at Sean and said, "If you think you're going to leave me there while you three go after these maniacs then you're crazier than a hoot owl. After what they did to me there isn't a snowballs chance in hell that I'm going to just call it a day and head back to the barn."

Annie spoke up, "Chet, I don't think you understand just how dangerous this is probably going to get. There's a pretty good chance that this could get violent. I don't think you're in any condition to come along on this mission."

"Dangerous," he said as his voice began to rise. "You don't think going off a cliff in a car or playing survival in the wilderness for two weeks with nothing but a home made spear and surviving on raw fish is dangerous?"

He was standing and pacing now. "Or coming face to face with a hungry wolf, or being chased down by a mad crazy moose is dangerous? And let's not forget about these assholes pounding me to a pulp and torturing me with a car battery. Oh, and I almost forgot, how about blowing me up!"

"I think that with all the fun I've been having, this mission is going to be like a walk in the park."

He paused for a moment to collect his composure. Then he continued, "Besides, you people need me. I grew up in this end of the country. I've been around these people all my life. I've watched these militia nut balls rant and rave about the government for all of my life. I've seen their camps. I've got first hand knowledge of how they train. I can blend in."

He sat back down on the log.

Annie looked over at Jake who said, "Sean, you know he's right. We could use his help."

Sean stood up and turned around taking a few steps away as he thought about it. He stopped, turned back and said, "Alright Chet, you can go, but only on one condition."

Chet looked up at him and beamed.

Sean held up his finger. "You have to promise me that you'll do exactly what I tell you to do. That means no heroics."

Chet nodded his head in agreement. "You got a deal."

Jake said, "and you have to help me make breakfast."

"As long as it's anything but fish," Chet smiled.

CHAPTER 21

May 14ᵗʰ
Hwy 95, Idaho

They had made their way via route 71 to hwy 95. They were headed back to Lewiston. Sean was driving and Annie was riding shotgun with Jake and Chet in the back seats.

Jake asked Sean, "So, what's the plan Sherlock."

"I've been thinking about it. Those guys at the Meth lab knew we were coming."

"Yeah, and,,,," Jake let his voice trail off expectantly.

"Someone had to have tipped them off."

"So who do you think told them?" asked Annie.

"Sean thought for a moment then said, "There were only a few people that knew we were there, and even fewer that knew we were with Homeland Security." He let that sink in for a few seconds.

"In fact there were only two people that knew it," Annie said starting to understand where Sean was going with this.

"Exactly," Sean said.

Jake sat in the back thinking and then, as if a light bulb went off he said, "The only two that knew were Ranger Mathews and the Sheriff."

Chet spoke up. "Wait a minute. You guys think Jack Mathews is involved in this?"

"It's got to be either him or the Sheriff," replied Annie.

"That seems impossible," said Chet.

"Yeah well my money's on Sheriff Wally. There was something off about him." This came from Jake.

"He did try awfully hard to convince us that there was nothing wrong with the water," said Annie.

"Well, in the interest of being thorough I think we should have a talk with both of them," said Sean. "And since we know where to find the ranger I think we should start with him first."

They pulled into Lewiston at about 2:30pm and headed straight for the Ranger Station. Chet was driving. They had each had a turn behind the wheel and Chet easily found his way back to the station.

They walked in and asked for Ranger Mathews. The clerk was a pretty young girl that didn't look old enough to drive. She smiled at them all, especially Jake who looked over at Annie and grinned.

"Please take a seat and I'll go tell Jack you're here," she said as she stood and walked away down a hall. She looked over here shoulder at Jake and smiled again as she disappeared around a corner.

Annie scowled at Jake and when the young lady was out of ear shot she said quietly, "Sixteen'll get you twenty." Then she grinned back at Jake.

A few seconds later the girl came back around the corner and approached them as she said, "Ranger Mathews will be right up."

She sat back down at her desk and continued working at her computer terminal.

It was only a few seconds and they heard footsteps approaching from down the hall.

As they watched Ranger Jack Mathews came around the corner and smiled broadly as he approached.

"Well, I didn't expect to see you folks so soon."

He looked over at Chet and held out his hand as he said, "Ranger Ellison, are you ever a sight for sore eyes. We pretty much had you figured as a goner. Shouldn't you be in a hospital or something?" He shook Chet's hand warmly.

"Please call me Chet," he said as he took the older man's hand. "I'm fine but there were many times out there that I started to figure myself as a goner."

The ranger's face darkened as he said, "I'm sorry about your partner. We took his body to the county coroner's office. He'll have to do an autopsy. You know DNA tests and that kind of stuff. It'll probably take a couple of weeks. We've notified his next of kin. I believe it was his sister down in southern California."

"Thank you Jack, I'm sure Andy would have appreciated your effort," Chet said with a sad expression.

The large ranger turned to the others and as if to change the subject he said, "So what brings you people back to our little community?"

Sean stepped forward and without preamble said, "Ranger Mathews, according to Chet here those guys at the Meth lab knew we were coming. There were only two people that knew what we were doing here and you're one of them."

Ranger Jack Mathews looked at all of them and said, "You think I'm the one that alerted them to your presents?"

"It had to be either you or Sheriff Murphy," Annie said as her cold glare locked on the ranger's eyes.

The big ranger stood there looking at each one of them. When his gaze got to Sean he said, "Maybe you can tell me why a National Ranger would do anything to help these radical nut jobs. Hasn't it occurred to you that helping these clowns fight against the United States Government would be like shooting myself in the foot."

Sean looked at Annie who looked over at Jake who shrugged his shoulders as he said, "He's got a point."

Chet watched as the tension of the moment dissipated.

Sean stood there for a moment and then asked the ranger, "What can you tell us about the sheriff?"

"Well," he replied as he thought about it. 'Wally's been the sheriff here for about seven years. He's been living here for about ten years. He started out as a deputy sheriff and was eventually elected sheriff after the other sheriff died in a hunting accident. He and Wally were deer hunting about fifteen miles out of town. They never found the hunter that actually shot him but Wally said there were a lot of hunters out that day. Hell, it could have been a stray bullet. The guy that shot him probably didn't even know he did it. The forest gets pretty thick out there."

"I can attest to that," said Chet and everybody smiled at him in sympathy.

"It was right after that that the county had a hurried election to fill the vacant spot for sheriff and the rest is history."

"Didn't anyone suspect that Wally may have been the shooter?" Annie asked.

"The folks in this part of the country tend to be real trusting of the people in law enforcement. It really never even crossed their minds to question Wally's story."

They all stood there for a moment and finally Sean said, "Sounds like it's time to go find the sheriff and have a little talk with him."

"Do you have any idea where we might locate the sheriff," he asked Ranger Mathews.

"Sure," he replied pointing toward the town. "This time of day he'll be down at the shooting range. It's about a mile and a half on the other end of town."

They all started filling out the door and the ranger said, "If there's anything I can do to help just let me know. Then as an after thought he said, "and Chet, it sure is good to see you're all right."

Chet smiled and said, "It sure is good to be back."

He shook the ranger's hand then turned and headed out the door.

They all piled into the car and Jake got behind the wheel. As he started the engine he asked, "Where to?"

Sean said, "I think it's time to go see Sheriff Wally."

They started driving through town keeping under the speed limit.

As they were going past the downtown area Chet who was riding shotgun suddenly yelled, "Jake, pull over!"

Jake immediately complied and looked over to see Chet turned in his seat looking out the rear window across the street.

Jake followed his gaze and said, "What's up Chet?"

They all turned and Chet said," That's their truck."

It was parked at the curb in front of bar. The sign above the door read Danny's Bar.

"Are you sure?"

"It's not the kind of thing I'd forget. White, with a primer grey right front bumper, that's theirs all right," he replied as he threw open the door and jumped out of the truck.

"Shouldn't we stop him," Annie said as they all piled out of the SUV and hurried across the street following Chet.

"I wouldn't miss this for anything," Jake smiled as they all hurried to catch up with him.

Chet reached the door to Danny's and swung it open. He stepped inside and stood there for a moment to let his eyes adjust to the bar's dark interior all the while scanning the room until his gaze locked on Charlie.

He was standing about halfway down the bar with his back to the door talking to the same two fat hippies from the mobile home. One of them must have said something funny and all three of them burst into laughter.

As Chet crossed the bar room in their direction Sean, Jake and Annie came through the door. The whole bar got silent.

The two fat hippies saw Chet coming toward them and Charlie, following their gaze, turned to see what they were starring at.

He saw Chet and stammered as if he were seeing a ghost, "You, it can't be. You're supposed to be dea..."

He never got a chance to finish his sentence. Chet hit him square in the face with every ounce of strength he had. Charlie's nose exploded in a spray of blood as he fell backwards to the floor. The two fat hippies jumped from their bar stools to come to the aid of their fallen comrade.

Jake, who was two steps behind Chet stepped around him and held out his hand to stop them with a shake of his head and a menacing look in his eye. The hippies froze and looked at each other not knowing exactly what to do.

At that point the bartender who was standing at the end of the bar reached under the bar and came up with a sawed off shotgun which he aimed at the side of Jake's head.

Annie, who was the last one through the door and was standing right next to the bartender, had her forty five semi-automatic out of her purse with such lightening speed that unless you were starring right at her you would have thought that she had the gun out before she entered the bar.

She jammed the barrel of the weapon into the bartender's left ear and screamed, "Freeze asshole, FBI."

The bartender lowered his shotgun and placed it slowly on the bar and stepped back.

Everyone in the place started to stand at once.

Sean who was halfway between Annie and Chet had fortunately had the sense to grab his own revolver from the glove compartment of the SUV. He pulled the gun from his waist band and fanned it around the room. Everyone sat back down. That is everyone except the two fat hippies. They just stood there starring at Jake the same way a rabbit would stare at a hungry fox. Charlie was still lying on the floor unconscious.

The door opened behind Annie and everyone turned to see Sheriff Wally walk through the door.

"What the hell is going on here?" he yelled.

Annie, using her left hand reached into her purse and pulled out her credentials shoving them into the sheriff's face while still holding the gun on the bartender.

"Sheriff, I'm with the FBI and I'm ordering you to arrest these three piles of crap," she said as she gestured toward the two fat hippies and the unconscious man lying on the floor in front of them.

"What's the charges?" he asked indignantly.

"Kidnapping, assault, attempted murder, possession of narcotics with the intent to sell and just plain pissing me off."

"You two," Chet said pointing at the two hippies and Charlie, "Pick him up and follow the sheriff."

"We'll be right behind you sheriff," said Annie as they watched them pick up the still unconscious man and head for the door.

Chet, Jake, Sean and Annie all backed out the door slowly making sure that no one like the bartender decided to come to the rescue of the three bad guys.

When they were outside they all walked over to the sheriff who was in the process of loading the three guys into the back of his cruiser.

Annie said, "We'll be over to interrogate those three in a few minutes."

Then, as an afterthought she added, "And by the way sheriff, don't do anything stupid like let them escape. That is unless you want to end up the focal point of a grand jury investigation."

CHAPTER 22

May 15th
Sheriff's Jailhouse
Lewiston, Idaho

"Just who in the hell do you think you are?" the sheriff roared as he stood behind his desk scowling at Annie who was standing on the other side of the desk with both of her hands on his desk leaning across toward the sheriff.

"This is gonna be good," whispered Sean to Jake as they watched from across the room where they stood leaning against the wall with Chet.

"I'll tell you who we are you pile of dog crap," Annie screamed as she leaned even closer into the sheriff's face. "We're the ones who were dam near blown up because some asshole decided to tell the Keepers that we were headed up the Snake River to test the water for contaminants."

"Now, we're going to keep those three dirt bags separated so that we can interrogate them and find out just what it is that the Keepers are up to. In the mean time my friend Jake here will keep you company."

She turned her back on the sheriff and faced Sean, Jake and Chet. She winked and said, "Jake, if this clown so much as looks like he might try to make a call, you have my permission to show him some down home justice."

Jake looked at the sheriff and gave him his most menacing smile as he said, "Yes mam."

The sheriff who had turned pale looked at Annie and stammered, "Y… your with the FBI. You can't treat me like this," as sweat began forming in his forehead.

"Ahh.. but sheriff, Chet and I don't work for the FBI," Jake said as he walk over to the sheriff and removed his side arm. "We'll just keep an eye on this for you, just in case.

Annie looked over at Sean and said, "Sean, why don't you come and help me with our three prisoners.

"Sure thing Annie," he replied. Then he looked over at Jake and said, "Now Jake remember, it's alright if you break a few bones but we have to keep him alive, at least for now."

The sheriff looked at Jake and Chet and swallowed hard as Sean and Annie left the room.

When they had closed the door behind them Annie asked, "Jake wouldn't really hurt him, would he?"

"Jake, nah, now Chet, I don't know about. He's been through a lot but I'm sure Jake'll keep him in check.

They walked down the long hallway to the interrogation rooms. They had the sheriff's key card and went to the first room which had hippie number one in it. As they entered the man looked up at them and gave them kind of a half smile. His eyes were darting around the room.

Annie and Sean sat down in the chairs across from him.

After just a few moments Annie said, "Allen," she had checked all of their IDs. "Do you know why you are being arrested?"

He looked down at the table and said quietly, "Because we was running a meth lab."

As he said that he looked up and grinned showing off his missing front teeth.

Sean was trying to figure out whether the drug use had caused him to lose his teeth or could it have been a fight. He decided it was most likely the later.

Annie looked him in the eye and said, "Yes that's part of it, but also there a few other charges that we're adding to the list. Would you like to hear what they are?"

He looked up at her and shook his head up and down. It gave him kind of a Jack in the Box clown look.

Annie looked down at him and said, "First, there's possession with intent to sell. Then there's kidnapping and assault with intent to do serious bodily harm. Then we have attempted murder with special circumstances. That carries a life sentence without parole. We also know that you're tied to the militia group known as The Keepers which we believe is attempting to commit an act of terrorism. That means that under The Patriot Act we can hold you indefinitely without parole."

As Sean watched it was almost comical the way Allen the fat hippie continued to stare up at Annie. Then his expression changed all of a sudden. It was as if a light bulb went off in his brain. One minute he was sitting there staring at her in a dope induced coma, and then all of a sudden a look of fear settled on his face. It was the same type of look that a small child would give a parent when he got caught doing something wrong. Then he lowered his head and began to cry.

Annie looked over at Sean and shrugged. She would have almost felt pity for him if it hadn't been for the fact that she knew what this scum bucket had done to Chet.

"I didn't mean to hurt that ranger guy." He blubbered as he continued to sob. "Charlie made us do it. He told us that if we didn't help him torture the information out of him that he would tell John Hamilton and John would have Hank Mire kill us in our sleep."

Sean stepped forward and said, "Who is John Hamilton?"

"He runs The Keepers, and he's one real scary dude," the hippie said. "Hank's his enforcer and he's almost as mean as Mr. Hamilton."

Annie looked at Sean and then asked Allen, "Has this John Hamilton killed other people before?"

"I've never seen him do it but people say he killed one girl for just smiling at a government guy, strangled her with his bare hands."

"Allen, you've been real helpful. Can you tell us where this John Hamilton is right now?"

"No, they don't tell me stuff like that." He sat there in thought for a moment. Then he brightened and said, "But Charlie might know. He knows a lot of things."

Annie said, "Alright Allen," She could see that his hands were shaking and he was beginning to pick at scabs on his arms. "You just wait here and I'll see if we can't send in a Coke for you."

She and Sean headed out the door and into the hallway.

As soon as the door was closed behind them she turned to Sean and said, "So, what do you think?"

"I think we better see if we can corroborate any of this information with his friend first and then have a serious talk with Charlie."

They walked down the hall to the next door and Annie checked her notes before they entered. "This guy's name is Harley Frank. It kind of makes you wonder if parents know when their child is born that he'll become one of these types of people so they pick their names to match their future line of work."

She stepped into the room and Sean followed closing the door behind him. He again assumed his position against the wall while Annie approached the second hippie.

He was a little larger than the first guy but he still had the same demeanor as Allen had. He slumped in his chair as if he already knew what she about to say. Buy the time she had finished explaining the charges pending against him and the information that Allen had already given her Annie and Sean could both see the defeated look on his face.

He basically repeated the same story Allen had told them including the fact that if they were going to be able to find John Hamilton the answers would have to come from Charlie.

When they walked into the room where Charlie Finley was he was sitting in the metal chair starring straight ahead with a defiant look on his face. He had a bandage across his nose which was broken according to Dr. Jerome Higgins, who was the local medicine man they had brought in to attend to him.

Annie and Sean each took a seat across from him and while Annie opened a folder she had brought with her Sean just sat there looking at him. He could see that Charlie was seriously pissed but there was something else there. As he sat there starring at him he saw a slight tick on the left side of his face. The anger was a façade to hide something else. This man was scared.

Annie started, "Well Charlie, you've been a very bad boy." His eyes moved to Annie.

"According to this," she tapped the folder for effect, "this isn't the first time you've been in trouble with the law."

She looked down at the folder and began to read aloud. "Assault with a deadly weapon, drug traffic, attempted rape involving a minor. You just can't seam to stay out of trouble. Now we've got kidnapping, attempted murder, assault with attempt to commit murder." She closed the folder and sat back. "Looks like your going to jail for the rest of your natural life. Which I might add probably won't be for all that long when I get done leaking word that you ratted out The Keepers."

Sean saw that she had hit a nerve. He said, "I wonder how long it'll take Hamilton to put out a contract on you?"

"You can't do that." He was beginning to sweat. "I haven't told you one dam thing," he proclaimed.

Sean leaned forward and said quietly with as much menace as he could muster, "You don't have to Charlie. Once the word gets out that you caved in and started talking you'll be lucky if you last a week. Hell, even if you were able to beat the charges on a technicality, your life isn't worth the stuff I scrape off my shoe after a visit to the dog park."

Annie leaned forward, "The only chance you've got is to help us find him so we can put him out of business."

"Forget it, I'll take my chances," he said without much conviction. He was really sweating now.

"You think about it," she said as she picked up the folder. They both stood and walked out of the room.

When Sean had closed the door Annie turned to him and said mockingly, "The stuff you scrape off you're shoe after a visit to the dog park?"

Sean smiled and shrugged, "I don't even have a dog."

They walked back up to the front office and found Jake and Chet.

"Where's our illustrious sheriff?" Sean asked.

"He's in the head. I don't think he feels all that good," said Jake with a grin. "So, what did you find out?"

Annie filled them in and as she finished the sheriff came out of the bathroom looking a little green around the gills.

A deputy came into the room and said, "That guy, Charlie, said he needs to talk to you two."

Annie smiled at Sean and they both headed back down the hall.

When they walked back into the room Charlie immediately began talking. He started by telling how he got involved with The Keepers and how he had been placed in charge of the drug operation in this area. He told them about other drug labs and their locations.

As it turned out he gave them a wealth of information. That is until they asked about "The Plan".

That was where the well of information dried up.

"Are you trying to tell us that they trusted you with millions of dollars worth of drugs but they didn't tell you all about this plan and what it was about?" Annie asked incredulously.

"That's what I'm trying to say," Charlie explained. "They kept everything a secret. They were afraid that if any of us found out about it and then they were caught, they might tell the Feds."

Annie looked over at Sean and shrugged her shoulders.

Sean stepped forward and said, "Charlie, I want you to take a minute and concentrate.

Do you remember anything, anything at all that was said when they got to the meth lab?"

"Well," Charlie said as he sat there thinking. He had a look on his face that looked half way between pain and constipation. "When they showed up, I did hear John whisper to Hank that they had to be real careful that the fed we caught wouldn't be able to mess anything up with the plan. That's why he wanted us to kill him."

"Did they say anything about where they were headed when they were leaving?"

"Hank did ask John just how long it was going to take them to make it to Calgary. Charlie said. "I think that's in Canada."

Annie stepped forward. "Did they say what they were going to do when they got to Calgary?"

"No, but while we was sitting on the porch havin a beerHank's cell phone went off and when he got done talkin he told John that everyone would be there for the meeting in two days."

"Did he say where the meeting was going to take place?" Sean asked.

"No, no he didn't." Charlie thought again for a few moments. Then he said, "You know, I was up there a few years back with John and a couple other guys from The Keepers. We went to a really nice place kind of out in the woods. It was a big place, you know, like a hotel. I think they called it a lodge. It was run by a feller, what was his name."

Charlie's face got all contorted again as he thought. "Johnson, that's it. Wayne Johnson. That's his name alright." He sat back and grinned at the two them triumphantly.

Sean looked over Annie and she asked, "Charlie, I want you to think real hard. Do you remember anything, anything at all that they said about Wayne Johnson or what they were planning to do when they got to Calgary?"

"Well, they said they were going to meet up with some other members so they could start the final preparations for "The Plan." He said this as he held up two fingers of each hand in the universal language for exclamation points. "They said that it was getting close and they had to make sure that everything was ready."

Then he sat back and asked, "Say, do you think I can get a Coke or something. I'm getting real thirsty."

"Let me see what I can do," said Annie as she and Sean got up and headed out the door.

"What do you think," Sean asked when they were clear of the room.

"I think I'm going to get on the phone to our Canadian friends and see if they can find out anything about this Wayne Johnson character."

"Yeah, and maybe I can call Washington and see if they can find anything on him," said Sean as they both pulled out their cell phones and headed for the front office.

When they walked in to the office, Chet was watching the sheriff and Jake was on the phone at the sheriff's desk.

"Ok," he said into the handset as he waved at the two of them. "We'll be waiting."

He hung up the phone and looked up at Annie.

"Man o'man, you sure have got some clout with the Lords of the G-men. That was the Boise field office of the FBI. When I first called they started to give me the runaround, that is until I told them that we were working with Angelina Cartier. Then the you know what hit the ventilator. They immediately switched me over to the head of station who in turn listened to what I had to say. He's sending four agents by jet helicopter to take care of deputy dog here and the three prisoners. He said they'd be here in about an hour and fifteen minutes."

"Good work Jake," said Sean. "We can hitch a ride in that chopper back to Boise.

From there we can arrange for a plane to Calgary."

Chet just sat there listening and then said, "Wow, you guys don't mess around do you?"

"Not when it comes to national security and a potential attack on the USA we don't. We're not about to get lethargic or complacent and end up with another Oklahoma City," Annie replied.

"Besides," Jake said, "All this sitting around babysitting is starting to get real boring."

Sean said, "Annie has to make a phone call to the Canadian Mounties while I call Washington. Jake, how about calling the Boise Airport and see if you can set up a plane while Chet takes sheriff Wally back to his own cell to wait for the agents from the FBI."

Jake stood up and removed the sheriff's gun belt. He held the gun and the belt out to Chet who took it and smiled.

"And Chet, maybe you better lock those other three in separate cells."

Annie called out, "Oh, and would you see if you can find them a Coke."

"I'll be glad to. Maybe I'll get lucky and one or two of them will try to escape."

This got Annie's attention as she watched him walk out of the office with the sheriff.

"You don't suppose," she thought out loud.

"Nah," Jake said, "probably not." He looked over at Sean and both of them shrugged.

As Annie and Sean came back into the office they heard the distinct whop, whop, whop, of the FBI helicopter as it made its approach to land in the front parking lot of the Sheriff Station. They saw Chet looking out the front window and Jake was just getting off the phone.

"Ok guys, the best I could do on short notice was a twin prop King Air."

"That'll work just fine," Sean said.

"Yeah, but the bad thing is it won't be available until tomorrow morning.

"Well," Annie sighed, "looks we're back to Boise's Hamilton Inn again."

"I'll go ahead and book our rooms," Jake said as he reached for the phone with a boyish grin on his face. "I'm mighty parched and I just happen to know a bartender."

He looked over at Annie who gave him scowling look. Then she looked over at Sean who was smiling at her, she couldn't help it and she laughed.

Chet, who turned from the window with a puzzled expression on his face asked, "Did I miss something?"

"I'll tell you on the way," Jake said as the FBI team walked in.

CHAPTER 23

May 15th
On the road from
Calgary to Spokane

John was surprised when his cell phone rang. He looked over at Hank as he retrieved it from his pocket.

He checked the caller ID and didn't recognize the number. He hit the send button and brought it up to his ear. Hank listened as he heard his boss say, "Yeah, who is this."

"Is this Mr. H?" the caller asked with a little hesitation in his voice.

"Who wants to know?" John answered irritably.

"Th…this is Dan Childers Mr. H. I'm the owner of Danny's Bar in Lewiston."

It took John just a moment to put a face to the name. He said joviently, "Hey Dan, what can I do for you?"

"We just had four armed people come in here. One of them, a woman, said she was from the FBI. They arrested Charlie, Allen and Harley."

John looked at Hank and shook his head. Then he said into the phone, "Dan, where was the sheriff while all this was happening?"

"He walked in at the end and the FBI lady shoved her badge in his face and told him to shut up. They all left here and headed over to the jail."

"Ok Dan, I'll look into it. In the mean time if you hear anything else be sure to let me know, you hear?"

"Yes sir," Dan said as he smiled to himself proudly.

John looked over to Hank again and said, "Looks like we might have a small problem."

He filled Hank in on what Dan had relayed to him.

"Those three idiots are dumber than a tree stump, and as far as the sheriff, he doesn't know anything about the plan."

"I know but you better call Wayne Johnson in Calgary and let him know what happened. Tell him to be ready just in case."

Hank reached for his own cell phone and started dialing.

Julie Delany and Anna Barnes were back in the bar looking for information about the Meth lab explosion when Chet had stepped into the bar and all hell had broken loose.

During the entire time they had pretended to cower while they both had their hands inside their purses wrapped around their hand guns just in case things went wrong.

Thankfully it hadn't been necessary to expose themselves.

Afterward they had stayed at the bar listening to the other patrons talking excitedly about what had happened. They were also hoping that they might hear something about who was behind the earlier explosion.

They did hear the speculation that the three that had been taken away had something to do with the drug world.

They just happened to be sitting two bar stools away from Dan Childers when he made the phone call to John Hamilton.

The two of them sat with their heads together acting like frightened young girls while they listened to one side of the conversation.

To them it sounded like he was informing someone very important about what had happened.

By the smile on his face when he finished the call, it was clear that he was pretty proud of himself.

They stood up and headed out the front door. They were sure that the phone call they had just heard could be very important to the home office and they needed to make a report of it.

As they started to walk away from the bar Dan Childers came up behind them and grabbed Anna's arm spinning her around roughly.

"You know I've been watching you two for the last couple of days and something just doesn't seem quite right. You always seem to be drunk but you rarely buy a drink."

Anna struggled and yelled, "Let go of me you bastard."

Julie who was a step ahead, turned and took one step back toward Dan and kicked him square in the crotch so hard that his feet literally left the ground. He immediately grabbed himself with both hands and let out a high pitch scream as he went to the ground.

Julie looked down at him and said nonchalantly, "The lady said to let her go."

They both laughed as they turned and walked away to make their report.

CHAPTER 24

May 15th, 2012
Boise, Idaho

The four of them stepped down from the Jet Ranger helicopter onto the tarmac.

Jake said to know one particularly, "I get the feeling we've been here before."

"No kidding," Annie said, "But at least this time we know a lot more than we did the last time."

"Well, hello again."

They turned around at once to find Cecil Barringer right behind them. "Couldn't stand to stay away I see?" he said lightheartedly.

Sean stepped forward and extended his hand. "Hello Cecil, we just couldn't wait to get another one of those fantastic meals." He turned and gestured toward Chet. "Cecil, this is Chet Ellison, of the National Park Service."

Cecil held out his hand as he said, "You're not by any chance one of the two missing rangers that we've heard about? It's absolutely remarkable that you were able to survive."

Chet blushed as he shook the agent's hand. "Yeah, I guess that would be me."

Jake chimed in, "Yeah, Chet here is a real mountain man, half man, half beast."

Annie took her elbow and jammed it into Jakes ribs. Jake winced as he said, "What did I say?"

She said to Cecil, "Chet had to show remarkable endurance just to survive like he did."

Cecil stared at Chet in admiration and said, "Remarkable, you'll have to tell me all about it at dinner tonight." I reserved a table at 7:30, if that's all right."

"That's perfect," said Sean. Then to Chet he said, "You're in for a real treat tonight."

"I'll go ahead and have all your gear transferred to the King Air. If you would all follow me to the Suburban I'll give you a ride to the hotel."

"Say, Cecil," Jake asked. You wouldn't happen to know if a young lady by the name of Jill is working at the bar tonight?"

"I wouldn't be at all surprised if she is."

Jake looked over at Annie and smiled ear to ear.

Sean walked up behind Annie and said quietly in her ear, "He's encouragable."

When they reached the hotel Cecil excused himself and went to the front desk to sign them in. When he returned he handed out electronic room cards to Annie, Sean and Chet.

"I'm sorry but they only had one more room available. It looks like you and Jake will be bunking together," he said apologetically. "But at least it has two separate queen beds."

He said this last statement with a slight grin that only Annie and Sean saw. They both had to turn away in order to hide their amusement.

Chet stood there holding the key looking at Cecil until Jake spoke up.

"That's ok Chet, I don't plan on spending a lot of time in the room anyway, if you know what I mean," smiling at Chet and moving his eyebrows up and down in a Groucho Marx imitation.

They all headed off toward the elevators telling Cecil that they'd meet him around 7:00 in the bar.

At dinner Chet recounted his survival adventure to Cecil and they all told him about the explosion and the subsequent events in Lewiston.

Cecil said, "You must be completely exhausted."

"I don't know about the rest of these people but I can say for myself that a good night sleep will be just what the doctor ordered," Annie said.

"What time are you expecting to take off in the morning," Cecil asked looking over at Sean.

"I'm planning on being wheels up by about 9:00am." Sean replied as he looked over at Jake.

"Don't worry Mr. Holmes, I'll be ready," Jake said defensively.

"I never had any doubt Mr. Watson. But just to be sure let's head up to my room to go over a little strategy tonight so in the morning we'll all be on the same page."

"That sounds like a good idea," said Annie as she also looked over at Jake. Then to Cecil she added, "You're more than welcome to join us."

"I think I should head back to the airport and make sure that everything is in order there."

"Ok, then I think I'll stop by my room and check in with the powers that be and I'll meet the rest of you in Sean's room," said Annie.

She stood up and headed for the elevators as the rest of them watched her go.

Chet said, "She sure has a lot of energy."

"Yeah she does," said Jake with a look of admiration. "She sure took over at that bar."

Sean said, "I sure hope she knows when to duck and run."

A few minutes later they were in Sean's room and they began listing what kind of ordinance they had and started going over some prelimary plans.

About a half an hour later there was a knock at the door and Jake answered it after checking the peep hole on the door. He stepped out of the way and Annie came in. It looked as if she had just stepped out of the shower. Her hair was wet and she wore no makeup and was dressed in one of the hotel complimentary bathrobes.

Sean looked up as she walked in and did a double take. She walked in with bare feet and was carrying her laptop computer under her arm. Sean thought she looked beautiful.

Jake, who never missed a beat, took one look at Sean, smirked and said, "I think I must be over dressed."

Chet looked up and saw Annie, then looked at Sean, then at Jake. He blushed and quickly looked down at the documents in front of him.

Annie said,"I took a quick shower after I spoke to Washington and while I did the Canadians downloaded everything they had on Wayne Johnson. I thought you all better get a look at this right away."

She sat down on the couch next to Sean and opened her lap top. All three of them looked at the screen as she read.

Report; 05/15/2010 21;30hrs
Johnson, Wayne James
AKA: James Wayne
James Broan
Donald Brown
Wanted for weapons trafficking, fraud, assault, attempted murder
Assessment rating; Very dangerous
Use extreme caution

Jake stood up straight and said, "This guy sure sounds like a serious player."
"If you think that sound like a problem, wait till you get a look at this."
Annie said as she clicked to a new screen. It read;

From; DEA 05/15/2010 17:10hrs
To; Angelina Cartier
Regarding; Militia activity
Danny's Bar, Lewiston, ID

Agent Cartier,
We received a message from two of our agents who were at the bar after your arrest. They happened to be sitting at the end of the bar and were able to hear part of a phone call that was made by the owner, a Dan Childers to a person he called Mr. H. It appears that he told this Mr. H about you coming into the bar and making the arrest. If you have any other questions you can reach me via e-mail. Good luck and good hunting.

"What do you think Sean?" asked Jake.

"I think we have to assume that Mr. H. has to be John Hamilton so he knows that we arrested those three idiots. We also have to assume that Wayne Johnson has provided Hamilton with what he needs to complete his plan. I think there is a strong possibility that

he may have figured out that his three flunkies could have provided us with a trail to Johnson and that he has probably already called him to tell him that we might be coming by for a talk. Given Johnson's background I think our mission has just gotten a lot more dangerous."

"Agreed, so what do we do now?" asked Jake.

"I think it's time for Annie to make a call to our friends in the Mounties and see if they can offer a little assistance."

"I'm sure that won't be a problem. If I know them, and remember that my father and brothers are all Mounties, their probably chomping at the bit to be a part of taking down this pond scum. They said they were going to meet us at the airport in Calgary tomorrow when we arrive."

Sean then turned to Chet and said, "You know Chet, you've already done more than your share of the heavy lifting. I'm sure no one would think any less of you if you bowed out of this one."

Chet straightened in his seat and said with a grin, "Are you kidding. I wouldn't miss this for the oil in Canada."

Sean looked around at the team and said, "Ok then, we're off to see the wizard."

"Not bad Sean. I like the simile. On that fine note I'm headed down stairs to see if I can locate a very lovely bartender," as Jake stood and headed toward the door he smiled and winked at Annie.

Chet stood next, stretched and yawned. "I'm headed for the best night's sleep that I've had in quite a while." He stood and followed Jake out.

Sean sat there on the couch as he watched Annie in her bare feet stand and head for the door. (If only, he thought).

When she got to the door she did something strange. She took the 'Do Not Disturb' sign and put on the outside of the door closed it and locked the dead bolt. Then she turned and walked back toward Sean.

He stood up as she came close and stepped forward to put his arms around her. He gently leaned forward and kissed her lightly on the lips. She smelled of vanilla bath lotion and he could taste a trace of chamomile tea and lemon on her lips. He pulled back from her. She wrapped her arms around him and kissed him hard on the mouth. As she did he could feel her tremble in his arms. She stepped back from him, undid her bathrobe and let it drop to the floor.

He lifted her into his arms, carried her across the room and laid her gently on the king size bed.

When Sean woke the next morning she was gone. He laid there for a few minutes savoring the memory of last night. He smiled, sighed and rolled out of bed heading for the shower.

CHAPTER 25

May 16th

On the road to Spokane, Washington

"Wayne, its John."

"Yeah John, what can I do for you?' said Wayne Johnson from his lodge outside Calgary.

John said, "I've just gotten word that our friends from the government have filed a flight plan from Boise to Calgary. According to the report their supposed to land in Calgary at about 1:00pm your time. Have you been able to gather everything you need for your party?"

"Sure have," he answered as he looked around the main room of the hunting lodge.

"I was able to get twelve of our people from Cochrane to come on down. They brought plenty of party favors too."

"That's great! I'll be sure to pass it on to our mutual friend. He'll be glad to hear it."

Johnson asked, "How many guests can we expect?"

"I understand that there are four of them. One of them is a woman from the FBI, two of them are scientists from Homeland Security and the last one is the ranger that we tried to blow up at the meth lab."

"I wonder why their bringing the ranger with them."

"Probably for revenge I'd guess."

"Well we'll make sure we give them a real down home welcome," said Johnson. "How are you doing with the rest of the operation?"

"We'll be in Spokane by noon tomorrow and then we can get everything in order for the final show."

"Will you be calling me to let me know what the final objective is? I'd sure like to know. In fact, if you can let me know soon enough I was sort of hoping I could fly in and be a part of it," said Wayne Johnson.

"I'll call you tomorrow afternoon and let you know, and why don't you bring along your friends from Cochrane."

"Ok, I'll be waiting for your call," said Johnson and he broke the connection.

John Hamilton looked over at Hank and said, "I think those government people are in for one hell of a surprise."

"Yeah, I sure would like to be there to see their faces when they get a look at what Wayne has in store for them."

John said, "I think that when they see what we have in store for them, the government is going to get a real good look at what happens when you piss off the people of this country. That should be quite a sight to see. Watch your speed. We don't want to get a ticket," he said as he looked at Hank and they both smiled.

CHAPTER 26

May 16th
Calgary Airport
Calgary, Canada

The sun was high in the sky as Sean taxied to the terminal designated for private aircraft. They were met by a stern looking uniformed man who came toward them as they stepped off the King Air. He was obviously from their customs department and he meant business.

He held out his hand and demanded their passports. Annie pulled out her FBI credentials and held them up for him.

"Do you think that means anything in Canada Ms. Cartier," He said with a fair amount of disgust in his tone and demeanor. "Hand over your passport immediately or I'll have you arrested."

"I don't think you brought enough manpower for that." This came from Jake who stood next to Annie.

"Let's take it easy folks," said Sean who was on the other side of Annie. "We don't want to start an international incident over this.

Annie glared at the officer and growled, "We don't have to take this crap from this overgrown Boy Scout."

Chet stood behind the three of them and just smiled.

The customs official's face flushed as he raised his right hand. From what seemed out of nowhere five SUV's came racing from the side of a nearby hanger with their lights flashing and their sirens blaring. The vehicles screeched to a halt and uniformed soldiers piled out of their vehicles and surrounded them as they pointed their M16s at them menacingly.

Annie started to protest and reach for her gun but Sean put a hand on her arm and shook his head.

They all stood there just starring at each other until the customs official smirked and said quietly, "I want all four of you to put your hands in the air and get down on your knees."

Jake said, "Why don't you get down on your knees and kiss my…"

"Jake," Sean said with a certain amount of urgency. "Maybe we should just do what the man says."

Suddenly they heard an engine revving and they all, even the soldiers, turned to see a car coming toward them from the main terminal. It had to be doing at least 120 kilometers per hour and it was flashing it's headlights.

Everyone watched as it came on so fast that at one point Sean thought it might ram the customs vehicles. It stopped just short of the group and as the passenger door flew open a very large and imposing man stepped out. He was dressed in a suit and tie and walked directly over to the customs agent. He towered over the smaller agent and said in a booming voice, "What the hell do you think you're doing here?"

He gestured toward the Americans and said, "These people are here at the request of the Prime Minister himself. He and the President of the United States have decided that their knowledge and expertise are necessary to accomplish a very important mission.

The customs agent paled immediately and looked over at the four Americans who were just standing there taking all of this in.

He said, "I don't know what to say."

The man in the suit went on, "I'll tell you what to say you fool. You tell your men here to stand down. Then you apologize to our friends here and then get in a car with your men and get the hell out of here, and don't forget to leave one of your SUVs' for our guests."

"P..P..Please forgive my aggressive behavior," he stammered as he turned on his heels and practically ran for the vehicles.

The large man in the suit stood there watching the customs people depart. Then he slowly turned back to the foursome.

As Sean, Jake and Chet watched, the man smiled at them, or more directly at Annie.

She looked back at him and to all of their surprise she shrieked like a child and ran to him throwing her arms around him and giving him a fierce bear hug and a kiss on the cheek. He hugged her back and kissed her on the cheek.

Sean felt a small twinge of jealousy as he stood there not knowing what to think.

"Jimmy, what are you doing here?" Before he could answer she whirled back around and declared, "Sean, Jake, Chet, I'd like to introduce you to my big brother Jimmy."

All of them stepped forward and shook hands warmly.

Sean said to Annie, "I had no idea that we would be greeted by one of your family members."

"Neither did I. Jimmy, what are you doing here?

"I was promoted to supervisor for the Calgary post. I've been assigned to assist you in any way possible."

"Well that was some line you gave that pushy little customs agent about the Prime Minister and the President being involved," Jake said as he grinned.

"That was no line Jake. The Prime Minister is taking a personal interest in this. You see, we've been after this Wayne Johnson for a good long time but we've never been able to build a decent case against him."

"It seems that your president telephoned our PM and personally asked for his help. He explained about this potential terrorist act and," Jimmy paused for effect, "Ta-da, here we are."

"Wow," Chet said. "The President of the United States and the Prime Minister of Canada know about this."

"You better believe it," Sean said. "You might think that these guys just sit in their fancy offices with their proverbial heads in the sand, but there is very little that gets past them when it comes to protecting their country against terrorists."

"That's a fact," said Jimmy. "That's why I've been instructed to help you."

"That's great," Sean said. "Is there someplace we can go and discuss our plan?"

"Sure, why don't you load your gear into the SUV and then you can follow me to my office."

Annie spoke up, "If it's all the same to you guys I'm going to ride with Jimmy. It'll give us a chance to talk."

"No problem Annie. Maybe you can start briefing him on what we're up against here," said Sean.

Annie and her brother headed for his car as Sean, Jake and Chet started pulling their gear from the King Air and stowing it in the back of the SUV.

As Jimmy and Annie sat in the car waiting for the guys to finish loading their SUV Jimmy smiled and said, "OK, so which one of those guys are you sweet on."

She playfully punched him in the arm and said, "That's none of your business."

"Come on Annie. Mom and Dad are gonna want to know when I tell them about you running around the western end of the countryside with these three."

"I think you should just keep that to yourself. Mom and Dad know I'm a good girl."

"OK," he said. "Besides, I'd put my money on that Sean."

She blushed and turned away.

"I thought so," he said as he smiled at her.

"I wonder what kind of help we're going to get from him." Chet said as he watched them walk toward the waiting car.

Jake said, "If he's anywhere near as formidable as his sister, it makes me feel a little sorry for this Wayne Johnson guy."

As they drove off following Jimmy's car, nobody noticed the wiry little man working on a Cessna 182. He was wearing a set of airport coveralls and a baseball style cap with the Calgary Flames hockey team logo on it. He watched out of the corner of his eye as they drove off. Then he walked away from the Cessna and casually headed for their King Air.

CHAPTER 27

May 16th
Headquarters, Canadian Mounties
Calgary, Canada

They were all in a conference room and were joined by Sergeant Allen Purcell of the hostage rescue section of the Canadian Mounties. This section was the same as their SWAT team and in fact used the same personal.

On the way back to Jimmy's office Annie had called the Washington office of the FBI who had in turn contacted the NSA and had obtained satellite images of Wayne Johnson's lodge. Everyone in the room was now bent over the table examining the photos.

"Man, by the number of vehicles at the lodge, it's either a convention or these guys know we're coming," said Jake.

"I would bet on the later," Sean said as he leaned even closer to the pictures.

Jimmy spoke up, "This is your party. How do you want to handle it?"

Annie said, "According to what we know about this guy, he makes his living selling weapons to anyone who is willing to pay the price. With that in mind we have to assume these nut balls will be armed to the teeth."

Jimmy said, "What do you think Sarg?"

"I think we treat it the same way we would in any other SWAT mission. We hit them at 1:00am in the morning just when their all getting sleepy. If we're lucky they will have also had some liquor. We use overwhelming force, speed and technology. I've got twenty very well trained agents on standby. I think they're the best in all of Canada."

"Ok then, I think we should let the Sergeant handle this, with one exception." They all looked over at Sean. "Jake and I will go in first and get as close as possible to Johnson before your guys start to take them out. Sergeant, it's important that each one of your crew get a copy of Johnson's picture. It's imperative that we take him alive. He's the only link we have to John Hamilton and The Keepers."

"Oh, no you don't Sean," Annie proclaimed. "You're not leaving me out of this party. I'm going in with you two."

"Annie, it's your job to stay at the command trailer with Chet and Jimmy and help coordinate this assault. You and Jimmy are both trained in these kinds of tactics and Chet knows how these country boys think. Besides, you know as well as I do that a small force has a lot better chance of getting through the main forces and getting inside close to Johnson."

Annie thought for a moment, and then conceded, "You're probably right, but if you go getting yourself killed, I swear I'll never talk to you again. And that goes for you too Jake."

Jake looked at her solemnly and putting his right hand over his heart pledged, "I promise not to let Sean or myself be killed here today."

Jimmy looked over at Annie and asked, "Hey sis, where'd you get these guys."

"You don't want to know," she replied shaking her head

It was 12:00 midnight when they all pulled off the main road and parked their vehicles in a small clearing about 200 ft. from the dirt road that led to Wayne Johnson's lodge which was about one and a half miles away.

"Ok," said Sergeant Purcell when they were all gathered. "Listen up people. Each person gets a secured headset with mike. You'll be talking to Agent Cartier so let's keep the chatter to a minimum. Report any bad guys and watch out for booby traps. You also want to make sure you've got your gas mask. Agents Malone and Collins will be going in ahead of us so let's try real hard not shoot them."

Jake leaned toward Sean and whispered, "He's just kidding, right?"

Sean shrugged his shoulders.

Purcell went on, "The snipers go in next. Let command know when you guys are in position. Everybody has night vision goggles so keep your eyes peeled for anything unusual. Let's move out."

Sean and Jake both slipped on their packs and placed their NVGs up on their heads. They turned to Annie, Chet and Jimmy who were all standing together and Sean smiled and said, "See you on the flip side."

Annie called out after them, "You two remember what I told you."

Jake turned and smiled, and then they were gone.

Chet turned back toward their command center and said, "We better get in there and do our part."

Sean and Jake had been walking for about 10 minutes before they got their first glimpse of the lights at the lodge. They started moving very slowly, both moving their heads back and forth scanning the area for any lookouts. Jake was in front of Sean and slightly to his left.

Suddenly Sean reached out and grabbed Jake's backpack and yanked him back so hard that Jake almost fell over backwards.

Jake looked at Sean and put both of his hands out palms up as if to say "What".

Sean leaned down and sprinkled a hand full of dirt across the path. Jakes mouth dropped open as he saw what had Sean so worked up. Cutting across the path was a very thin wire.

Sean keyed his mike and quietly said, "Everybody keep alert. We just came across a trip wire. It looks like it's a bobby trap. It's wired a claymore mine, pretty nasty trick."

Annie came on the air into everyone's ear, "You heard him folks, take your time and be careful."

Sean and Jake worked their way closer to the lodge. They stopped at the edge of the tree line about 100 feet from the house. The house was dark except for one light in the center of the front of it. They both assumed that the lit room was a living room. They still had their NVGs on as they scanned the rest of the house. They switched to infra-red and were able to pick up the heat signatures of people in the house. They counted seven people that were not moving and appeared to be in a horizontal position presumably sleeping.

There was one figure at a window in what looked like an attic looking out. One of the prone people was in an upstairs corner room that seemed much larger than the rest of the rooms. Sean and Jake looked at each other and Jake whispered, "Johnson." Sean shook his head in agreement. They both continued scanning.

Sean reached over and touched Jakes forearm and gestured toward the front corner of the house where he had spotted another guard. They both moved back into the tree line and made their way around the house. Sure enough they located a century at each of the corners and one just inside the back door. That made twelve guards plus Johnson and all of the guards appeared to be armed with MP5 machine guns.

They started to move back toward the tree line very slowly. Suddenly Sean stopped. He slowly began moving his eyes across the compound. Then he froze.

"What is it Sean," Jake asked.

Sean's reply was just one word and it made Jakes blood run cold. He quietly said, "Dogs."

Chet who was listening in the command post looked over to Annie and said, "Did he say dogs?"

Annie turned pale and stared at the monitors. There were five helmet mounted cameras but all of those were being held back until Sean and Jake were in position.

Jake began scanning the area looking for the direction the attack would come from. He caught movement from the north side of the house and realized immediately that they were Dobermans. They weren't going to be able to out run them. He saw both of them running at full speed right toward them. He could make out their white teeth and it looked as though they were snarling. They were obviously well trained because they weren't barking, but it was easy to tell that they meant business.

Sean whispered quietly, "Move back into the trees, slowly."

Jake did as he was told but his mind was telling him to get the hell out of there. As he moved back he looked over at Sean and saw that he was starring straight at the animals. He almost looked like he was in some sort of a trance. "Sean, are you all right?"

Sean held up his hand in a way that told Jake he was concentrating. The dogs were closing fast. When they were about ten feet from Sean they suddenly stopped and sat down.

"Dam," Jake said quietly to no one in particular. "He did it again."

Annie who was listening at the center sat back in her chair and sighed in relief. Chet and Jimmy both looked at Annie and Chet asked, "What just happened?"

Annie glanced over to them both and said, "I'll tell you later."

Sean approached the two animals and gently patted them both on their heads. He then held his hand palm out to tell them to stay, and then pointed his index finger to the ground and the dogs laid down. He patted them both on their heads and looked at their collars. "Jake, meet Rocky and Sugar Ray."

"Good doggies," said Jake as he cautiously walked around the animals.

Sean motioned for Jake to follow him and he began to make his way to the side of the house crouching as he went.

Jake reluctantly followed but as he passed the dogs he was keeping one eye on them and the other eye on the house and the guards.

Sean had picked a spot at the house that was screened off from the rear guard by a large fire place. They could also see some light coming through a window which was almost directly over their heads. When they reached the building, Sean radioed that they were in position. He also relayed the position of the guards.

He leaned over and whispered into Jake's ear, "When the fun starts, we go through the window and head for the stairs. You look front and I look back."

Jake smiled and nodded his head in understanding. Then they waited.

CHAPTER 28

May 16th
Wayne Johnson's Lodge
Calgary, Canada

It was about fifteen minutes later and all six of the snipers had assumed their positions. The rest of the assault team had made it to the tree line. Half of them were in front and half were in back. When the command was given Sergeant Purcell was to call out to the lodge on a megaphone and demand that they give up peacefully.

Purcell called command and told them that all was ready. He was given the 'GO' command and raised the megaphone to his lips.

"Johnson, this is the Canadian Mounties. We have the lodge surrounded. Throw down your weapons and…"

That was as far as he got. The attic window exploded outward and immediately the guard inside that window began hosing down the area with automatic gun fire. The Mounties had expected this and had already taken cover in the tree line.

As soon as Sean and Jake heard the gun fire they both took three steps back from the house and charged the window.

Annie who was standing now in the command center spoke into her headset, "Command to snipers, you are clear to engage. I repeat, you are clear to engage."

As Sean and Jake broke through the window into the living room of the lodge, Jake who was looking to the front of the room spotted the man at the front door. The guard turned at the noise of the shattering glass and was bringing his machine gun up to shoot when the side of his head seemed to explode in a spray of blood and bone.

"Let's hear it for the Mounties" Jake said as he turned to follow Sean who was already headed for the stairs.

They heard the report of several high powered rifles then Annie's voice came again over their headsets, "Ok people, let'm have the gas."

Sean and Jake reached into their backpacks and produced their gas masks which they donned immediately. At that same moment they heard the distinct WHOMP- WHOMP and the gas canisters crashed through the windows all around them.

The house started to fog up immediately from the gas. They both ran for the stairs.

When they reached the top step they started down a hallway leading to the room they believed Wayne Johnson was in. After just a couple of steps a door flew open about ten feet in front of them and a man dressed in his boxers stepped into the hall holding a large caliber automatic pistol in his hand.

He spotted Sean and Jake and started to raise his gun. Sean yelled out, "No," but the man's hand continued to come up. Sean's shot hit him in the shoulder and the 357's impact spun him around as the automatic flew from his hand. He went to the floor grabbing his shoulder and screaming in pain.

Jake said to Sean, "Now that's what I call getting caught with your pants down."

They continued on down the hall headed for the set of double doors at the far end.

When they got there both of them leaned their heads against the doors and listened.

After a moment of not hearing anything Jake looked at Sean and they both shrugged.

"Sounds like nobody's home," said Sean. He reached down and slowly began turning the door knob while Jake readied his pistol. Sean slammed open the door and they both vaulted into the room, Sean low and Jake high. The room was empty.

They began walking around the room. As Sean passed a large book shelf on the wall opposite the bed he looked down at the floor and could see where the dust on the floor had been disturbed. Using hand signals he called Jake over and pointed to the floor. Jake immediately recognized what he was looking at.

Again he held his gun in the ready position and Sean pulled on the side of the shelf. It pulled out easily revealing a stairway headed down. They both listened and they could hear footsteps going down in a hurry. Without any hesitation Sean took off down the stairs in pursuit with Jake right on his heels.

The stairs led all the way to the cellar and when they got there the room was dark. The only light was coming from two small cellar windows high on the wall. They could just make out the figure of a man running away from them headed for a short set of stairs leading up to a set if double storm doors.

"Hold it right there Johnson," yelled Jake. The man reached back with his right hand and fired a shot from a pistol. The shot went wide and into the side of the furnace. Jake heard an ear piercing whistle from behind him and just as the man went up the stairs and opened the doors two snarling beasts hit him square in the chest.

He went flying backwards as his gun flew from his hand. He screamed and the two Dobermans went down on his chest as he slid back down to the basement floor.

The dogs stood over him as Jake walked over to where he was lying and in his best country boy accent said, "Well looky what we got here. Mr. Wayne Johnson just dropped in to say howdy."

Sean walked past them and stepping up the steps closed the doors. He turned and without saying a word the two dogs sat down on each side of Johnson. He said, "We don't have a lot of time so I'll get right to the point."

Jake picked up on Sean's meaning and immediately moved to cover the door.

Sean's expression turned sinister as he said to Johnson who was still lying on his back between the two dogs, "I want you to tell me where John Hamilton is and what his plan is."

Johnson looked up at Sean and grinned like a Cheshire cat. He pointed up at him and said, "Rocky, Sugar Ray, Krieg."

Jake said, "Sean, my German's a little rusty but I think he just told those two dogs to attack you."

The dogs just sat there looking at Sean.

"Krieg, Krieg," Johnson repeated as he raised his voice. Then seeing no response from the animals he raised his right hand to strike Rocky.

It happened so fast you had to be paying close attention to even see it. As Johnson struck out at the dog, Rocky snapped at his forearm. There was an audible 'crack' as the bone in his arm broke.

Johnson let out a howl and grabbed his now broken arm and cradled it in his lap. "You can't do this. I have my rights. What have you done to my dogs?"

Jake said, "I'd say they're tired of the way you treat them."

Both dogs went to Sean and sat down on each side of him. "I'll asked you just one more time, where's Hamilton?"

Johnson looked up at him and said without a lot of conviction, "Piss off."

Sean looked down at the two dogs and both of them stood up and started to move forward as they rolled their upper lips back barring their teeth and growling menacingly.

"Ok, ok," Johnson said as he recoiled from the dogs. "I don't know what John Hamilton's master plan is. He kept it secret from everyone except Hank I think. He said he was going to reveal it to the rest of his crew when they met at the warehouse in Spokane."

"We'll need that address."

"2710 Washington St., it's in the middle of the industrial section of the city. Now help me please. I need a doctor."

They heard a vehicle approaching and Jake went over and opened the cellar doors. Annie got out of the vehicle and looked around to access the situation until her gaze settled on Jake who was waving her over.

Annie headed in toward him with Chet and Jimmy following. When she got close Jake turned and headed back down the stairs with the other three following. She walked down the stairs and when she got to the bottom she surveyed the area and saw Wayne Johnson lying on the floor. He was white as a ghost and holding his right arm. She could see the bone of his forearm protruding from the skin.

She turned and said accusingly, "Jake, what did you do to him? You should know that torturing information out of a suspect is usually followed by the suspect getting all charges dropped."

Sean stepped out of the shadows and said, "We didn't touch him."

"Oh really, then who did that to his arm?" she spat out angrily.

"They did," he said as he pointed to the corner.

Annie's eyes followed Sean's arm and she shined her light on the two dogs. They were both sitting on their haunches with their tongues hanging out looking about as proud as two pups under a red wagon.

Sean said with a little to much flair, "I'd like to introduce you to Rocky and Sugar Ray. Boys I'd like you to meet Annie." Then he lowered his voice and told the two animals in a hushed voice, "Be careful guys, she's with the FBI, you know, the cops."

The two dogs immediately lay down.

Jake spoke up, "Annie these dogs are his," He said pointing to Johnson, "or at least they were his. I don't think they like the way he's been treating them."

Two uniforms came down the steps and Jimmy told them to take Mr. Johnson into custody and reminded them to read him his rights which weren't many being that Canada took it very personally when someone was suspected of being a terrorist.

For the next five minutes Jake and Sean explained what happened and told them about Spokane.

"I think we better hurry if we expect to do anything to stop these crazy bastards," said Annie. Then she turned to her brother, "Can you clean up this mess so we can try to catch up to them?"

"Hey, no problem sis," he replied as if he'd just been asked to take out the garbage, which when he thought about it wasn't a lot different.

"Thanks Jimmy," she said as she reached out and hugged him. "We better get moving," and they started back up the steps.

She said her goodbyes to Jimmy and they all headed for the SUV. When they were almost there Chet asked, "Hey Sean, what about Rocky and Sugar Ray?"

As Chet went around to the side door and got in Sean opened the back of the truck and whistled. Both dogs came out of the basement like they'd been shot out of a cannon and jumped up into the back of the vehicle. By the time Sean got in the dogs were doing their best to give Chet a bath while he was smiling like a kid at Christmas.

Sean said, "Well, it looks like these two guys just found their new best friend."

CHAPTER 29

May 17th
Warehouse
2170 Washington St.
Spokane, Washington

All eyes were on the table in the middle of the room that was covered with a sheet as John Hamilton called out to get everyone's attention.

"All right everyone, pay attention. I don't want to have to repeat myself." He said this in a way that left no doubt in anybody's mind that to make him repeat himself could be very detrimental to your health.

Behind him leaning against the wall stood a man that no one had ever seen before but it was obvious that Hamilton was not the one in command.

Hank stood on the other side of the table, and as John nodded, the two of them lifted off the sheet. Beneath it was a scaled down replica of an industrial complex. It didn't take anyone very long to see the seven steam towers of a nuclear power plant. They all looked at each other pensively as John began.

"As you can see our target is a nuclear power plant. More specifically it's the Columbia Generation Station in Richland, Washington."

Red Dunn spoke first, "John, isn't a nuclear power plant pretty much impregnable to attack?"

"The main plant is protected to the point where it might take a nuclear explosion to damage it however as we learned in Tokyo after that earthquake the biggest Achilles' heel of the nuclear power plant is the ability to use fresh water to cool the fusion rods."

"We intend to take out the water lines that provide the cooling for the fusion rods. As you can see if we blow these lines," he said pointing to the large pipelines heading into a structure at the South East corner of the complex. "We will effectively remove the water coming from the River. In doing this we can prevent them from cooling the rods. This will cause a catastrophic failure of the entire cooling system which in turn will cause the release of radioactivity both into the atmosphere and into the river effectively sending the radioactivity both East and West at the same time."

Jimmy Lyden spoke up, "John, what you're proposing could kill, or should I say would probably kill over a half million people in Portland and possibly many more from the surrounding area along the Columbia River. Not only that but assuming the wind blows from West to East it would probably contaminate who knows how many thousands of square miles of land in the Pacific Northwest possibly even all the way to the Rocky Mountains."

John looked at Jimmy and then almost imperceptibly glanced over to Hank who was standing at the other end of the table. He said," Jimmy, it sounds as though you're having second thoughts about what we're trying to accomplish here."

Jimmy locked eyes with John said," I'm all for the cause but I don't think it would serve our cause properly to offer up such wholesale slaughter. What you're talking about could very well turn public opinion against us in a big way."

John looked over to Hank and gave him a slight nod. Hank reached to his back and pulled out his 45 clock and shot Jimmy between the eyes.

John looked around the room and asked, "Is there anyone else here that isn't fully committed to this plan?" He looked at all the faces of the other people that were standing around the table. No one said another word.

John began to lay out his plan as if nothing had happened. "When we pull up to the main gate the front van will take out the guard. There's only one there. One of you will go into the guard shack and open the gate for the rest of us. As we enter the complex that same lead van will veer off to the left and cover the front of the main building here." He used a laser pointer to show them.

"This is where the main contingent of guards will be coming from once we're discovered which probably won't be long because the security cameras are all linked to the main command center inside this building.

It's important that the eight of you either kill them or at the very least keep them pinned down in there."

"The other two vans with the C4, each with two people in them, will follow us to this point," he said as he pointed to an area between the main building and another long building on the side. "One of the vans stays here with Hank and sets up their explosives to blow these two twenty four inch main water lines. These lines are the emergency water lines to cool the fusion rods in case of a failure of the condenser that's used to cool the rods. The other van follows us around to the rear where the condenser is house in this building." Again he pointed to a building that sat behind the main building.

"We all set our timers for thirty minutes on my mark. Does everyone understand?" He looked around room and everyone nodded their heads to the affirmative.

"Any questions?" Again he surveyed the room.

"All right then let's gather our gear and get in the vans, we've got a long ride ahead of us."

John watched as they all gathered their equipment and made for the three white vans waiting by the door of the warehouse. John and the man who was standing in the background went to the black suburban and got in as Hank made his way to the driver side. Hank hit a button and the roll up doors to the warehouse began to open. When it was open far enough they led their entourage out the door and headed south.

CHAPTER 30

May 17th, 2012
Calgary Airport

The sun was just starting to rise in the eastern sky as the six of them (the four of them and their new K-9 partners) pulled into the private aircraft section of the Calgary airport. They had made good time getting back due to Jimmy arranging a police escort all the way.

Sean wasted no time performing a pre-flight inspection of the King Air and within twenty minutes they had filed their flight plan and were in the air heading for Spokane. After they had reached an altitude of twelve thousand feet Sean set the plane's auto pilot and stepped back into the rear section of the aircraft.

He had a stern look on his face as he said, "I think it would be an understatement to say that I'm pretty sure Hamilton knows we're coming."

Annie nodded her head in agreement saying, "I've been in touch with Washington. They are in the process of getting a team together and organizing state and local police for help. What's our ETA into Spokane?"

"We should be there in about two hours," he said.

"That should work out just about right. They've also got a six man contingent from the FBI that has already left Seattle. They should get to Spokane just a little after we do."

Jake spoke up, "I just hope we get there in time to stop these maniacs before they do something that we'll all regret."

"Jake, why don't you and Chet take the time to check our weapons while we have a little time to kill, no pun intended. Chet, how are our two newest members of the team doing?"

Chet looked back at the two Dobermans that were each lying on a pair of double seats sound asleep. "Looks to me like their natural born flyers."

"Well I'd say they earned their beauty rest. If it wasn't for…….."

Sean's voice was interrupted by a sharp bang that seemed to come from the port side of the aircraft.

They all looked out the side windows and Jake said, "What the hell, did one of the wings fall off or something?"

"I don't know," Sean replied as he bolted for the cockpit with Jake right on his heels.

By the time Jake got seated Sean was scanning the gages as the plane leaned hard to port.

Jake said in his Dr. Watson voice, "I say Holms, what seems to be the problem."

"We've lost the prop governor on the port side. The propeller is flat blading," he said as he pulled back all of the power to the port engine. "We're going to have to put it down," he said as if he were explaining the intricacies of making a meatloaf.

He was in the process of fighting the yoke to bring the plain back to level as Jake immediately started scanning the area for a place to put the plane down.

Annie and Chet both stuck their heads into the cockpit just in time to hear the last part of the conversation and they both began scanning out the windows as well.

"There," Chet cried out pointing out to the right.

Everyone looked to where he was pointing and saw a dirt road that cut through a wheat field about a quarter of a mile away.

Sean said, "Well, that'll have to do. Ok, everybody strap yourselves in tight. It looks like it's going to be a ruff landing. Jake you better get to the back too."

"There isn't a snowball's chance in hell that I'm going to miss out on a front row seat to see this wreck," Jake said. "Besides, who else is going to be able to pull your smoking dead body out of this tin can?"

"Thanks for the vote of confidence."

"That's why you keep me around," he said as he looked over and smiled at Sean.

Sean began going through his landing procedures as he continued flying away, downwind from the landing spot. When he thought he was far enough away he began his turn to crosswind while at the same time lowering his flaps ten degrees and feathering power to the good engine.

He turned to final approach, put in full flaps and pulled back all of the power until the plane became a glider.

"I don't know why but I liked it a lot better when I could hear the engine," Jake said as he looked out the front window at the postage size makeshift runway.

"A lot of pilots call the propeller a fan because when it stops turning everybody starts to sweat. Oh crap," Sean said as he looked up from the gauges. "We're too high. We have to loose altitude in a hurry or we'll over shoot the runway. We've only got one shot because there's not enough power to go around for another approach."

With that Sean stomped his foot down on the left rudder pushing it all the way to the floor. The plane literally turned sideways as it continued to move forward toward the little runway.

Jake who was calmly watching said, "Well, that's sure to wake up the passengers."

Annie and Chet who were already nervous, clutched their armchairs with white knuckles as they felt the plane turn sideways and it began falling out of the sky like a rock.

Chet glanced back to check on the dogs and couldn't believe they were still sound asleep completely oblivious to what was happening.

Up in the cockpit Sean said calmly, "Timing is everything," as he continued sharing his time between the altimeter and the approaching runway.

When it seemed like the ground was impossibly close he pulled his foot back off the rudder and it almost seemed like the plane new exactly where the runway was. He pulled back on the yoke and flared the nose of the plane to make a perfect landing.

He was shutting down the equipment as Jake said in a loud voice, "Ladies and gentleman, we'd like to welcome you to the beautiful state of

Washington and thank you for flying Rent a Wreck Airlines. Please place your trays up and pull your seats to the upright position.

Sean said, "Now that was fun."

Chet opened the door and let the stairs down then climbed down and held his hand out for Annie. The dogs came bounding out next never touching a step. Jake and Sean came down and they all stood there for a moment and just looked around. In every direction the only thing they could see was wheat.

Annie said as she turned toward Jake, "Toto, I don't think we're in Kansas anymore."

Sean said, "Annie, you better get on the horn to the Seattle FBI and see if we can have their chopper stop by on the way and pick us up. While you're doing that I'll call the FAA and report that we made it down alright. Jake, you better get a hold of the guy you rented this bird from and let him know where he can find it. Tell him to bring a mechanic and a replacement prop governor. Chet, you keep an eye on our two four legged friends and make sure they don't eat the farmer that owns this farm."

Annie stepped back down the steps from the plane, "I spoke to the head of station. He said his guys had made good time from Seattle and were about five minutes from Spokane. He said he'd have the chopper refueled immediately and head back to pick us up. They should be here in about an hour and a half."

"That'll have to do," said Sean with a worried look on his face. "I just hope it'll give us enough time to catch up with these guys."

Everyone sat on the side of the road next to a small culvert and waited. That is everyone except Chet and his two buddies. He had found out that Rocky had a fondness for chasing rocks and wherever Rocky went Sugar Ray was right on his heels.

"Guess that explains how Rocky got his name," said Jake as they watched the dog fetch and retrieve.

At about one hour 25 min. after they had made contact with the FBI Sean stood up and looked to the East. He could hear the faint whop whop of an approaching helicopter in the distance. They all stood and watched as the helicopter approached and made a landing on the road stirring up massive amounts of dust and small rocks forcing them to turn their heads away.

As the rotors wound down they all grabbed their equipment and ran for the helicopter throwing everything inside and then jumping up into the side door and throwing it closed. The agent inside handed each of them a set of headsets and as Sean put his on he could hear Annie telling the pilot to take off as quickly as possible and head for Spokane.

An hour and a half later they were at Spokane Airport. As they landed they could see at least a dozen police cars from state and local authorities as well as a couple of black SUVs that obviously were FBI. The police were all in swat uniforms with Kevlar jackets and helmets. The FBI all were wearing their company issued parkas with Kevlar jackets and ball caps all with the company logo stenciled in bright yellow.

Annie took a moment to introduce herself and the rest of their team to an officer who identified himself as Captain Dean Blackburn of the Spokane Police Department. He was a short stocky man with hard eyes dressed in a plain business suite. It was obvious the guy was not messing around. He took a moment and informed them that the building at the address she had given them from Calgary was under surveillance and up until two minutes ago no one had been spotted arriving or leaving from it.

Annie and the rest of her team turned immediately, picked up their gear and headed for the SUV that only had one person sitting behind the steering wheel. The other five agents were in the other vehicle and as soon as they were ready all of the vehicles moved out with the Spokane police cars leading the way.

Within ten minutes they were completely surrounding the warehouse where they hoped they would find The Keepers.

This time it was the captain who spoke through the police cruiser's loud speaker. "This is Captain Blackburn of the Spokane police department. Come out of the building with your hands in the air." He waited for a full minute, then brought the mike back to his lips and said in an even more severe voice, "I repeat this is the Spokane Police Department. You have thirty seconds before we open fire."

They waited twenty seconds and then the captain began counting down, "Ten, nine, eight, seven six."

A smaller door to the right of the large truck doors slowly began to open. All around you could hear the audible sound as every officer racked a round into the chamber of their weapons.

As they watched they saw a set of hands stick out of the opening. Then they heard a voice cry out "Don't shot, don't shot."

While all weapons were trained on the door they saw an old man appear holding his shaking hands in the air.

"Hold your fire, I repeat, hold your fire," said Captain Blackburn.

Two officers rushed to the man from each side of the door and grabbed both of his arms pulling them behind him and hand cuffing him.

There was a sigh of relief that came almost in unison from the officers.

Sean, Jake, Annie, Chet and the two dogs were behind their SUV and Jake said, "Wow, I thought John Hamilton would be a lot younger."

"And a lot taller too," added Chet.

Annie ignored them both and said, "I think we better get in there and have a look around."

CHAPTER 31

May 17th
Washington St. Warehouse
Spokane, Washington

After questioning the old man as to whether or not there was anyone else in the building and being assured that there was not, they entered the building.

It was dark and cool in the warehouse as the four of them with the two dogs entered. Captain Blackburn followed and went right to the control switch for the large overhead door and as he pushed the up button the door began to open flooding the warehouse with light.

The six FBI men also came in with the old man in tow. They had removed his hand cuffs.

"What's your name sir?" asked Annie.

"B-Bernie Knoll mam, I mean officer."

"Well Bernie, My name is Agent Cartier and I'm with the Federal Bureau of Investigation. Why don't you tell us who you are and what you know."

"Well Officer…I mean Agent Cartier," he started out nervously. "I'm kind of the maintenance man around here. That is, it's sort of my job to keep things clean and make sure that the plumbing and electrical are all working properly so if the company that manages this place wants to show it to a potential renter everything will be in working order."

"So what were you doing in here?" Annie asked.

Bernie, looking embarrassed looked down at his feet and said, "Well, I started pretty early this morning and around eleven o'clock I decided to lay down on an old couch that's in the back behind some boxes. I guess I must have dozed off. The next thing I know I hear the big door opening and three white vans and a black SUV come rolling in then close the door behind them."

"Did you get a look at the people in the vehicles?"

"Sure did. There was about twelve of them that were all dressed up like soldiers, you know, with helmets on. And they were wearing those special jackets that are supposed to stop a bullet."

"You mean flak jackets?" Sean asked.

"Yeah, that's it, flak jackets. And there were six other dudes with them. The first one, the biggest one, did all the talking. He looked real mean. Then the second one, he wasn't quite as big as the first guy but he looked almost as mean. There were three others that seemed to stand out from the soldiers" He thought for a moment and then said, "Then there was a sixth guy that stood off to the back, not far from where I was. He seemed different that the others."

"What do you mean by different?" Annie glanced over to Sean, Jake and Chet.

The old man went on, "I don't know, he was just different that the others. He seemed calmer. It was almost like he didn't belong."

The four of them thought about that for a moment.

Then Sean asked, "Could you hear what they were talking about, what they were doing in here?"

"They were all standing around the table and then one of them started to argue with the big guy they called John. This John guy asked him a question, I think he called him Jimmy, and then the other mean looking guy pulled out a gun and shot Jimmy right between the eyes." The old man was obviously shaken. "When I saw that I got so scared that I almost messed myself. I got down behind the boxes and stayed there until I heard the police yelling."

"Where is the table that they were all standing around?" asked Sean.

The old man pointed to the other side of the warehouse. "Over there," he said.

They all looked in that direction and started to walk over to the table that could see on the opposite side of the large building.

Sean stopped and turned back to the old man. "When did they leave?"

"It was about three hours ago," replied the old man.

Sean looked at his watch, It was three thirty.

As they all approached the table they each saw the man the old man had referred to as Jimmy. He was lying on the floor just to the side of the large table. Surrounding his head was a large pool of blood. He was obviously dead.

Chet was just staring at him with Rocky and Sugar Ray sitting on either side of him. The two dogs wined quietly. "These people are animals," he said softly lowering his head.

"Well, I hope these animals aren't as smart as I'm afraid they might be." This came from Jake who was looking down at the table.

Sean was looking at the same thing.

Annie came over and said, "What is this?"

"This," Jake said pointing down at the model, "is a model of a fricken nuclear power plant."

"It's the Columbia Generating Station in Richland."

"Richland, Washington?" asked Chet incredulously.

"One in the same," answered Sean. "Jake and I took a tour of it a couple of years ago."

"Holy shit," Annie said as her hand shot to her mouth. "You don't think these wackos would actually try to damage a nuclear power plant do you?"

As they stood there looking over the model of the power plant Annie said, "So you're telling me that they could actually do serious damage to a nuclear power station?"

"What I'm saying is that it's possible but it would take a lot of explosives and they would have to be placed in very strategic places to do major damage," answered Sean.

"Excuse me," they heard Bernie say as he approached from behind them staying as far away from the dead man lying on the ground as possible. "I heard those guys talking about what they had in the vans."

"What did they say?" asked Annie.

"They said they had half a ton of C4."

Annie was speechless. She looked over at Sean and Jake who were bent over the table examining the model as if it were a priceless gem.

Sean said nonchalantly, "That doesn't come as much of a surprise. They'd need that much to do any real damage."

Annie said, "What does that mean, and how did they get that much C4 in the first place?"

Sean looked up at Annie. "It doesn't matter how they got it. What matters is the fact that they have it and if they have figured out how to use it to do the most damage."

"Where do you think they would use it?" she asked as she looked down at the table with a feeling of dread.

Sean looked over at Jake and both of them said at the same time, "The cooling system."

Jake said, "These plants use a basic heat exchanger system a little like your home air conditioner. They take water that's in a sealed system and pump it into a pond that keeps the reactor rods cool. The cool water goes in and as the fission rods cool the water becomes warm. Then the water is pumped back out through a condenser where it's cooled down and then pumped back into the pond to repeat the process. The cooling causes steam and that's what you see coming from the large stacks. If they blow up the condenser the process is interrupted, then the rods begin to overheat."

Chet spoke up, "Wait a minute, I thought all of the systems in these plants have backup systems in case of failure."

"That's the beauty of these plants. Their built close to a water source. Their backup system is the Columbia River," said Sean. "If the condenser goes down they can pump the water through these lines," he pointed to the two large pipes on the side of the main plant. "They can pump cold water in from the river to cool the pipes going to and from the pond. It's a basic circulation system. The water goes in one line and is returned with the other one."

Jake said, "There is one potential problem. If they blow the water lines from the river the whole system would be without any way to cool the rods and what your left with is a meltdown, similar to that movie The China

Syndrome. The rods become unstable and you have no choice but to release radio activity into the atmosphere."

Annie looked at them, "Oh my God," was all she could say.

Sean said, "There is one other potential problem."

They all looked at him.

"If they only blow the water feed line to the plant it's possible the return line that takes the water back to the river could begin to pump contaminated radio active water back into the Columbia."

It took Annie a moment to process what Sean was talking about.

"That means it could contaminate the Columbia River all the way to the Pacific Ocean?"

"That's right. That would endanger the entire City of Portland not to mention the damage it would do to the eco system for the entire northwest."

After a minute she said, "We've got to find a way to stop them."

All of a sudden everything was happening at once. While Sean and Jake studied the locations of the critical areas Annie was on her cell phone calling for the jet ranger helicopter to be ready for an immediate departure.

The FBI agents were stowing their weapons in one of the SUVs while Chet was loading the dogs into another one.

Annie got the police captain to give them a police escort to the airport and as Sean and Jake ran for the car and jumped in they were off.

When they got to the airport it looked like a fire sale. Weapons and agents piled into the jet ranger and as the door was pulled closed the helicopter leapt into the air and headed for Richland.

Annie had the copilot patch her through to the state police and she briefed them about what was happening. They said they would get the local police and get to the power plant immediately.

The copilot informed her that they were about twenty minutes from the Columbia Generating Station.

She informed the rest of the group. As she told Sean he looked at his watch and she and Jake could see the look in his eyes. This was going to be close.

CHAPTER 32

May 17th
Columbia Generating Station
Richland, Washington

It took about two and a half hours to reach Richland. They probably could have made it in two hours but John figured it wasn't a very good idea to go speeding down the highway at seventy or eighty miles per hour with four vehicle full of illegal weapons, not to mention the thousand pounds of C4 explosives.

When they pulled up to the main gate, the guard held up his hand as if to say halt. They were all dressed in their military gear so when they stopped in front of the guard he bent down and said, "Heah guys, what's up."

The guy in the driver's seat waited until the guard bent down, then he shot him in the face. One of the militia men in the rear jumped out and went into the shack. A moment later the gate blocking the entrance began to slide open.

The four vehicles went through the gate and as they drove toward the main reactor the lead vehicle turned into the parking area directly in front of the main door and took up their positions to guard against the security people that were sure to show up very soon.

The other two vans which had the explosives followed the SUV to the side of the reactor building. The first van had Al Jesop and Red Dunn in it along with two of the militia men. They parked almost directly beneath two enormous pipes that ran from a tower on the right into the side of the building. The pipes spanned about forty feet and were about twenty feet off the ground.

So far they hadn't ran into any other security people. As a matter of fact they hadn't seen anyone at all. John and Hank got out of the SUV and as the two soldiers in one of the vans started to set up two large extension ladders John looked around and smiled. "I love it when a plan comes together."

When he was sure that Al and Red knew where to place the charges for the best possible effect he got back into the SUV and he and Hank along with the other man and two additional soldiers headed around to the rear building with the last van full of explosives.

As he stopped at the door of the rear building and got out two men dressed as lab techs came out the door. One of them looked at John and the other men and immediately asked in a tone of superiority, "Who are you people and what are you doing here without a security escort?"

John looked at him and smiled. "We're the new lab technicians. The company sent us to replace you."

John pulled his MP5 around from his back and shot both of them in the chest. They both went down instantly clutching their chests. John walked over to them pulling his semi-automatic.

"You're both fired," and he shot both of them in the head.

By this time they could hear automatic gun fire coming from the front of the main building.

"Sounds like the guards decided to come out and play," said John as he went to the back of the van and began helping the other two guys start unloading the explosives. "We better get hustling before they call in every cop in the area."

They took the C4 into the building and followed John as he walked through the machinery to where the condenser was located. John, Hank and the other man started setting the explosives while the other two men found a shop dolly and headed back out to the van to get the rest of the C4.

As they worked John began to whistle. The other man said, "You really do enjoy this don't you."

"And why shouldn't I? The dam government has been a menace to me all of my life and you know what they say, payback's a bitch."

The other man said seriously, "John, we're not doing this for revenge. We're doing this to show the people of the United States that the government does these things without giving a dam about the people or the environment."

"Well good for you, but I'm just thinking how much fun it's going to be watching all those city slickers die a slow death."

As they kept setting the explosives the other two guys got back. They were out of breath as one of them said, "That gun fire's getting real loud out there. It sounds like the guards got some reinforcements."

"Well then don't just stand there. Get you buts moving and help us set up the rest of this so we can get the hell out of here," yelled John over the noise of the machines.

When they were done, John got on the radio and called Red.

"How are you guys doing on your end?"

He heard Red's voice sounding a little winded, "We're all set here. John we better get moving. It's starting to sound like a war zone out here."

John could hear the gunfire in the background. "That's an awful lot of fire power from just a hand full of security guards."

"They must have called in the local and state cops because there's more showing up every minute, Red yelled into the radio. What do you want me to do?"

"I want you to set the God dam charges on my mark. Set them for thirty minutes. That'll give us time to get clear of this place before the explosion. On my mark, three…two…one…mark."

John did the same with his timer. His radio cracked to life again. "Do you want us to go around to the front and help the rest of our people?"

"Screw them, they knew what they were getting into from the start. Send the two guys with you around to the front to try to help them. I'll send these two also. Then I want you to get your ass back here and we'll get the hell out of here."

"Roger that," he heard Red say.

CHAPTER 33

May 17th
Columbia Generating Station
Richland, Washington

As the helicopter approached from the northwest they could see the muzzle flashes from both the militia and the police. Police cruisers were spread out all across the front of the main reactor building and they could see more coming down the road leading into the plant.

When they flew over the guard shack they could see the dead guard lying on the pavement. They also saw both guards and militia people on the ground in front of the building.

They flew over the plant and saw the two water lines that fed from the river. Behind the building they saw the two dead technicians in front of the door leading into the rear building.

"That's where the condenser is located," said Jake into his headset.

"They all listened as the pilot said, "We're going to have to set down about five hundred feet behind the rear building in an open area."

"That'll have to do," Sean replied through his own headset. Then he turned to the rest of the group. "I think as soon as we set down we should split up. You guys," He pointed to the six FBI agents, "go around the north side of the main building and help out the police and guards in front. They won't expect anybody coming from that direction and you'll be closing in from their flank."

He looked over to Annie and Jake. "I think it would be best for you two to head for the water lines that come from the river. Jake knows where they're at and hopefully you'll be able to deactivate any bomb they may have set there. Chet and I will head for the condenser and see if we can find any explosives there."

He then spoke to everyone. "Everybody keep a sharp eye out. The bad guys that started all this are still in there somewhere."

Everyone nodded in agreement and the helicopter began to drop to the ground.

John, Hank and the others had just come out the door of the rear building as they heard and then saw the helicopter pass overhead.

"Shit," John exclaimed as he walked over to the rear of the SUV. He reached inside and pulled out an aluminum suitcase, laid it on the ground and opened it. Inside there was a tube packed in foam rubber. He pulled it out and quickly expanded the tube and raised it to his shoulder pointing it at the descending helicopter. He pulled the trigger half way waiting for the high pitched tone that told him that the surface to air missile was locked on target. As soon as he heard the tone he mashed the trigger all the way. Instantly there was a woosh and the missile shot from the tube headed for the doomed aircraft.

Hank said, "I don't think we're going to be able to get out through the rear."

"That's just great," said Red Dunn. "Now what are we going to do."

"Not a problem Red," John said casually. "We just split up and head for the side exit that's on the southeast corner of the complex. You and Al head around the south side of the pump station and the three of us will go around the north side where the pump lines are. That way we can check and make sure that no one's messing around with our bomb."

Red and Al both shook their heads in agreement and they all headed in their own directions.

The helicopter was about one hundred feet off the ground and descending when they heard the pilot yell out over the headsets, "We're being painted. "Shit, they've got a lock. Everybody hold on. This is going to be close."

Everyone in the bird felt their stomachs lurch as the pilot banked hard right. They heard the co-pilot call out frantically, "I've got a missile in the air."

The pilot pulled the helicopter hard left and everyone on the right side of the ship could see the missile bearing down on them. They watched it as it just missed the skids on the bottom and went right past them. It flew about one hundred feet and hit one of the reactors steam towers where it exploded in a huge ball of fire. The concussion hit the helicopter and spun it around one hundred and eighty degrees.

It seemed to fall out of the sky and when the helicopter hit the ground with a teeth jarring impact everyone just sat there for a moment waiting for the explosion that they were sure was coming.

The inside of the helicopter immediately filled with the smell of burning wire as smoke bellowed from the front of the bird.

"Everybody out," Sean yelled out over noise of the motors winding down.

Sean and Jake practically pushed Annie and Chet out the door with the FBI agents. The two dogs didn't need any persuasion. After they were sure everyone was clear of the smoking cabin the two of them climbed forward to help the pilot and the co-pilot out.

When they got to the cockpit the pilot was bent over holding his knee which was bent at an awkward angle. When he looked up it was obvious he was in tremendous pain. As Sean and Jake entered he said through gritted teeth, "One of you guys help Jimmy." He was referring to the co-pilot who was still belted in. He was out cold with his face covered in blood.

Sean said to Jake, "You get the pilot out of here and I'll take care of Jimmy."

Jake reached over and literally pulled the pilot back through the opening to the main cabin as the pilot groaned in pain. The cockpit was quickly filling with black smoke as Sean unsnapped Jimmy's seat harness and dragged his limp body out of the seat and back into the cabin.

By the time they reached the outside of the smoking helicopter the pilot had passed out from the pain. Sean and Jake carried the two men clear of the wreckage and gently laid them on the ground just as the helicopter burst into flames.

The six FBI agents took off immediately headed around to the front of the main building. It was obvious that these guys knew all about the Keepers and couldn't wait for the chance to take them down. They were finally going to get their chance.

Jake and Annie headed around the east side of the condenser building which would take them to the side of the main reactor building and the two large water lines.

Sean, with his face covered in soot, took Chet and headed to the west side of the building which would take them to the door to the condenser building where they had seen the two down lab technicians. Of course they also had the two Dobermans with them.

As the three of them jogged around to where the two pipe lines were John and Hank stopped and turned around to see the other man standing there looking confused.

"What the hell's wrong with you?" John asked.

"I forgot my backpack on the side of the building. When we came out and started talking I set it down next to the building. I've got to go back and get it. There are papers in it that will identify us."

"Well you better get your ass back there and get it. You can catch up to us at the pipe lines, but hustle up."

He turned and took off at a run back the way they had come.

John and Hank turned and started jogging to the water lines.

Sean and Chet got to the side door of the condenser building and found the two technicians lying face up on the ground. Both had been shot in the chest. It was also obvious that they had also been shot in the head point blank, executioner style.

Sean and Chet both had their guns out. Chet had a nine millimeter Glock and Sean had his trusted 357 magnum.

Sean said to Chet, "You wait here for the dogs and I'll go in and make sure that there's nobody inside. If you hear any shooting get in there and help me."

"Will do," Chet replied as he racked a cartridge into the chamber.

Annie and Jake were just coming up on the water lines when they spotted John Hamilton stepping down off a ladder that went to the overhead water lines. At the bottom holding the ladder was Hank Mire. They both had their backs to Annie and Jake.

Annie took up a two handed firing position as she yelled out, "FBI, freeze, hands in the air."

Jake, who had stepped to the side to put some space between he and Annie, had his MP5 aimed at Hank.

Hamilton continued descending the ladder to the ground and started to smile. "You two must be a couple of the government people that have been dogging us from the meth lab. Am I right?"

Annie took a step forward and repeated, "I said put your hands in the air and get down on your knees asshole.

John looked down at his feet and said, "Such terrible language. You know Hank, that's the problem with the government nowadays. They just plain don't have any manners. They don't know how to say please."

He kicked the base of the ladder and it began to topple over. At the same time Hank threw himself to the ground and rolled coming up with an MP5 of his own and was bringing it to bear on Annie. He moved remarkably fast for a man of his size. But he wasn't fast enough.

Jake, who was ready for the move raked the front his body with his machine pistol before he could fire. The impact hit Hank like a train, throwing him backward. He was dead before he hit the ground.

At the same time John Hamilton reached to his back and produced a 45 semi automatic of his own. As he brought it around Annie shot him in the heart. He dropped like rock.

Jake who was standing eight feet away said, "That'll to put a crimp in his master plan."

Annie said, "Come on, let's get that ladder back up there and take care of that bomb."

Meanwhile, as Chet stood in front of the door to the condenser building watching for the dogs he heard a man's voice from behind him.

"Hello Chet, long time no see."

Chet spun around and his mouth dropped open. "Andy?" He took a step forward. "It can't be."

He started to walk toward him. Then he saw the gun in Andy's hand and stopped.

"Andy, you died in the car crash. They said they found your body." Chet was still trying to come to grips with what he was seeing.

"Oh, they found a body all right. It just wasn't mine. It belonged to some tweeker that the Keepers had lying around. He was about my size and physical build so they took him and dressed him up in my cloths and put him on the side of that ravine. The animals did the rest. By the time they get the DNA results it'll be way too late."

"I don't understand. What are you doing here?" Chet asked.

"John Hamilton is my brother."

"But Andy, I've known you for years. You've been to my house. You've ate dinner at our table. You're no murderer."

"Don't you see Chet? We've got to stop the government from destroying the environment. They don't care. To them it's just the money. Nothing else matters to them. If we can't show the people of this country what the government is doing and make them understand there won't be anything left." He thought for a moment and then said, "Chet, it's not too late. You could join us."

Chet could see it in his eyes. There was something deranged about the way he looked. He decided to give it one more try.

"Andy don't you see that if you damage this nuclear reactor you could be condemning thousands, maybe hundreds of thousands of people to a painful death and that's not to mention that you could do irreparable damage to the same environment that your trying to save?"

Andy was shaking his head. He had tears in his eyes. "You just don't understand do you. Sometimes it's necessary to have sacrifices to help the greater good."

He raised the gun and pointed at Chet's face.

As Chet saw the gun come up he pleaded, "Andy you don't have to do this."

"It's too late, good bye Chet." He began to pull the trigger.

Chet saw the movement out of the corner of his eye. Sugar Ray was snarling and bearing down on Andy at full speed. Andy saw him at the same time as Chet and turned the gun toward the dog and fired. He caught

Sugar Ray in the right flank. The dog yelped as the impact of the bullet slammed him to the ground.

Chet, in a fit of rage, move in on Andy who immediately aimed the weapon back at Chet's face. He never saw Rocky. The dog lunged at his arm snapping his powerful jaws as he growled.

Andy, trying to keep his arm out of the dog's teeth pulled away as he shot at Chet. The shot hit Chet in the shoulder and spun him around. Then Andy turned around to face the attacking dog and raised the gun over his head in an attempt to hit the dog with it.

Sean heard the first shot from inside the condenser building and instead of going directly out the same door he used to enter the building he went around to the side exit. He went out and moved to the corner of the structure and looked out to see a man with his back to him raising a gun toward Chet. He also spotted Sugar Ray lying on the ground and saw Rocky barreling down on the gunman. The gun went off and he saw Chet spin around. The man raised the gun into the air to use it as a club on the dog. Sean stepped around the corner and yelled, "STOP".

The surprised man turned toward him and was moving the gun to aim at Sean but he was too late. Sean shot him between the eyes.

Sean stepped forward and stood over the man. Chet walked over to them holding his left arm.

Sean asked, "Who was he?"

Chet looked down at him and replied sadly, "That was Andy Franklin. He was my friend."

Chet moved quickly over to where Sugar Ray was lying on the ground and knelt beside him. The dog was still breathing. Sean walked up and Chet asked, "Is he going to die?"

Sean knelt down and put his hand on the dog's side. Rocky came over and sat next to Chet. He wined and licked Chet's face.

Sean said, "No Chet, he's going to be fine."

Then Sean stood up and said, "But none of us are going to be fine if we don't get in there and disarm that bomb."

Chet stood up and they both hurried into the building leaving Rocky who lay down next to Sugar Ray.

As they entered the building Chet asked Sean, "Have you found the bomb yet?" They had to yell to be heard over the noise from the machinery.

"Yes," Sean yelled. "It's attached to the electrical panel that feeds power to the condenser. If it blows that condenser won't be coming back on line for a very long time."

Chet followed Sean around several turns in the path that led through the maze of piping and equipment. When they rounded the last turn Chet stopped dead in his tracks.

He was looking at a huge machine. On the side of it he saw a large control panel. All around it there were blocks of what looked like putty, similar to the putty his children played with when they were younger. Only these blocks of putty were about two or three times bigger. And there were a lot of them.

They completely surrounded the control panel. There were hundreds of them. Attached to them there were a mess of wires that ran from small pencil like sticks that were stuck into the putty. All of the wires seemed to run back to a box that was stuck on the front of the panel. The box had a red LED that said 5:23 and was counting down. 5:22…5:21…5:20…

Sean pulled out his Swiss Army Knife and immediately started removing the four screws that held the front of the box's cover. As he worked Chet kept an eye on the LED. 4:36…4:35…4:34…

Sean lifted the cover up and Chet held it open as Sean began gently pulling out the maze of multi colored wires. 3:11…3:10…3:09…

"How are you going to figure out which wires to cut," Chet yelled into his ear.

Sean glanced over to Chet and couldn't help but notice the beads of sweat breaking out on his forehead and upper lip. He wondered briefly whether Chet might be

going into shock from his bullet wound. Then he followed his eyes to the LED and realized it had nothing to do with his shoulder. 2:17…2:16…2:15…

When Sean had most of the wires out of the box he found the set of them that went to the back of the LED. 1:42…1:41…1:40…

There were four of them. They were black, white, red and green. The problem was he had no idea which wire to cut. He held the scissors of his Swiss Army Knife in his hand and looked at Chet in hopes of spiritual guidance. Chet looked at him and just shrugged his shoulders. 0:51…0:50…0:49…

(Well, what the hell), he thought to himself. (Nothing ventured, nothing gained).

(Red means stop). He gently moved his scissors to cut the red wire. He was just starting to put pressure on them when a hand reached from behind him and gently took the scissors from his hand.

It was Annie. She moved the scissors to the green wire and cut it.

Sean and Chet both flinched reactively.

The LED read 0:17 and stopped.

Sean leaned back with a sigh of relief and said into her ear, "How did you know which wire to cut?"

"They teach us that in spy school," she said with a smile and a twinkle in her eye.

CHAPTER 34

May 28th
Memorial Day
Bend, Oregon

Julie Ellison stood at her kitchen sink washing the morning dishes. She could hear the children upstairs banging around trying to get ready to head downtown with her to the annual Memorial Day Parade.

Word was that as usual, pretty much the entire town was going to be there.

Julie was having a hard time getting excited about it. It had always been a tradition for her, Chet, Daniel and Alice, to go to the parade as a family.

They would all get there early enough to be able to set up their folding chairs and get a front row seat on Main Street.

After the parade they'd walk on over to spend the day at the park in the center of town with all of their friends. They'd eat hot dogs, hamburgers and corn on the cob. Then the kids would play games like the three legged race and the egg toss.

They'd listen to the country band and everyone, including the kids, would dance away the afternoon.

At night there was always a huge fireworks display and they'd lay down on their blanket and oooh and aaah at the sight of it all.

Julie just couldn't get excited about going to the activities this year. She hadn't heard a word from Chet in two weeks and she was worried sick. She knew he was doing something dangerous for the government.

Why couldn't she have married a plumber or an electrician like her father had told her? No, she married Chet, a forest ranger of all things.

She remembered the day they got married like it was yesterday. The plans they had made. The things they would do to make the world a better place to bring up their children.

But now she didn't know if her husband was dead or alive.

He hadn't even been able to tell her what he was up to. For all she knew he'd been eaten by a bear.

While she stood there, almost in tears, she looked out the front window to see a black SUV pull up at the curb in front of their house and her stomach jumped up into her throat.

(This was it,) she thought. The moment she was dreading. The moment when a man dressed in a black suite would get out of the car and walk up to her door and ring the door bell to tell her that her husband was dead.

A man in a black suite got out of the front seat and looked up at the house. Julie thought she was going to pass out. But then he did a strange thing. He went to the back door and opened it. A man stepped out of the car. He was wearing blue jeans and sneakers. He had on a tee shirt that had a yellow smiling face on it. Right below the face were the words,"Have a Nice Day". His left arm was in a sling.

There was something very familiar about this man. She did a double take and then it registered. It was Chet.

She ran to the front door, threw it open and bounded down the steps.

Chet ran into her open arms. When she hugged him fiercely he felt the pain of his wound shoot up his left arm but he didn't care. He was home.

She was smothering him with kisses and then he saw the kids. They were screaming, "Daddy, Daddy," as they ran down the steps across the yard and into his arms. They were all hugging each other and all talking at the same time.

It was at this moment when Julie remembered his arm. "Chet, what happen to your arm?"

"It's a long story and I'll tell all about it later, but first I've got a couple of friends I'd like you to meet."

They all got quiet and turned to the SUV. Chet whistled and Rocky and Sugar Ray came bounding out of the vehicle. They made it about half way up the lawn and Chet held out his hand and they both sat down.

"Guys, I'd like to introduce you to Rocky and Sugar Ray. Sugar Ray's the gimpy one."

Sugar Ray had a large bandage on his front left side.

Chet went on, "Boy's, meet your new family."

The kids let out a squeal and ran to the two big dogs that in turn licked them both in the face excitedly.

Alice yelled, "Daddy can we really keep them?"

"For as long as they want to stay."

Julie said quietly, "Chet, I don't know about this. Are they house broken? Are they safe?"

Chet smiled and turned toward the dogs. "Rocky, Sugar Ray, come over here and meet the boss." They both immediately walked over to Julie. They walked around behind her, then came up along side of her and sat down, one on each side.

Julie looked down at them and then said to Chet sarcastically, "Now you're going to tell me that they understand what I'm saying."

"Try saying something to them, you know, like give them a command."

She looked at him as if she were trying figure out whether or not he was pulling her leg. Then she looked back down at the two dogs and said quietly, "Rocky, Sugar Ray, lay down." The dogs immediately laid down."

She said, "Roll over," and they both rolled over on their backs. Then she tried to trick them by saying, "Sugar Ray, sit up."

Sugar Ray immediately got up to a sitting position while Rocky stayed on his back starring up at her. "Rocky you can sit up too." The dog complied.

Julie looked over at Chet who was standing there grinning from ear to ear. "That's amazing," was all she could say.

"Honey, you'll never have to lock your door again," he said.

"How many tricks do they know how to do?"

Chet said, "These are not tricks. I have it from a very well connected source which I'll explain to you later, that these two guys actually understand what you're saying."

As Julie stood there looking skeptical, Sugar Ray limped up to her and licked her hand. She said, "Oh, all right. But you two have to take care of them," she said to the kids.

Daniel and Alice screamed with delight and the dogs ran to them licking them both in the face.

Daniel asked, "Daddy can we take them with us to the parade?"

"I don't see why not, after all, their part of the family.

The kids cheered and Daniel said to the dogs, "Did you guys hear that. Come on Rocky."

Alice said, "Come on Sugar Ray."

They all headed up to the house. Chet leaned down and kissed Julie. Then he said,-"It's good to be home."

EPILOGUE

May 28th, 2012
Bourbon Street
New Orleans, Louisiana

They had spent the last nine days in a basement at the Federal Bureau of Investigation being debriefed about The Keepers and what had happened to the four of them.

Chet had been patched up and they had been questioned, first individually for hours at a time, and then collectively.

They were asked questions that they could not possibly know the answers to. Questions like do you know who will be taking over as their leader now that John Hamilton was dead. How many people are involved with the Keepers? When they shot and killed the people at the power plant did they identify themselves according to proper procedures?

It seemed to go on forever.

They asked Chet how Andy had faked his death and how had he become involved with the militia group.

Chet told them, "I had no idea that Andy had anything to do with them until he came up behind me at the nuclear power plant and told me that John Hamilton was his brother. Up until that moment I thought he had died in the car crash."

At one point there was some talk about pressing charges against him for his actions in the forest before Sean, Jake and Annie found him at the meth lab.

Once it was pointed out that he played a significant role in preventing a nuclear disaster, it was decided that Chet Ellison was a national hero and that he would receive a commendation and a promotion as well as a substantial pay increase.

When the debriefing was finally over Sean, Jake and Annie decided a well deserved vacation was in order. They ask if Chet wanted to join them but he said that he was real anxious to get home to see his family.

Because they only had the long Memorial Day weekend before they had to report back to their prospective jobs they decided on New Orleans.

The entire city was celebrating the holiday with a Jazz Festival. What could be better than The Big Easy during a Jazz Festival?

Sean borrowed a friend's Cessna 410 and they flew out on Saturday around noon and arrived in New Orleans at about 2:15pm.

They taxied to the private aviation portion of the airport and were met by a limousine from The Marriott Hotel.

They checked into their private suites at the front desk and on the way up Annie asked Sean, "Where did all this come from."

"Compliments of the very thankful and appreciative United States Government," replied Sean.

Annie looked at him suspiciously and said, "Well I know that my boss would never authorize something like this."

Jake spoke up, "No he wouldn't. But your boss's boss would."

Annie just looked at both of them for a moment and then she lit up, "You mean the."

"That's right, the big man himself."

All Annie could say was, "Wow".

They decided to meet in an hour in Annie's room and then decide what to do. When Sean and Jake got there Annie said, "Well, what do we do first?"

Sean said, "It's about 4:00 now. The jazz festival doesn't start until 8:00 and it's too early for dinner."

Jake spoke up, "I know a place on Bourbon Street that has a great happy hour."

Sean looked at Annie and raised his eye brows as if to ask, what do you think.

"Sounds good to me, let's go.

Fifteen minutes later they were at a hole in the wall bar right in the middle of Bourbon Street. True to his word, Jake ordered them all a beer and when the waitress brought them instead of bringing three, she brought nine beers.

When Annie told her that they had only ordered one a piece the waitress smiled and said, "It's happy hour. That means you buy one and you get two free."

Jake said, "See, I told you they had a great happy hour."

The place was filling fast. It seemed that the students from Alabama State had the weekend off and had decided to come to New Orleans to celebrate. By the time the DJ took the stage at 5:00 the place was packed.

At first Sean could see that Annie was getting a little anxious about the crowd and was about to suggest that the go somewhere else when the DJ took the stage and said,"It looks to me like the good state of Alabama is missing some of its scholars."

The crowd cheered and Sean saw Annie look at the cheering people around them and she smiled.

The DJ went on, "I think I've got just the song to get this party rocking." He reached down and a second later they all heard the beginning notes of Lynyrd Skynyrd"s Sweet Home Alabama.

There was a roar from the crowd and the place went crazy. They were all on their feet. The place was rock'n.

Annie looked over and saw Jake with a college coed up on his shoulders. He looked at her and grinned ear to ear.

Annie said, "Oh, what the hell." She stepped up on a chair and swung her leg over Sean's shoulder and slid herself up.

An hour and several beers later they were walking out of the bar and headed to get some dinner before the festival. They headed west down Bourbon Street. None of them seemed to notice the two guys across the street watching them.

They didn't see them, but Sean felt them.

THE END